THE TURTLES OF
TASMAN

JACK LONDON

1st WORLD
LIBRARY
Literary Society

The Turtles of Tasman

Jack London

© 1st World Library, 2006
PO Box 2211
Fairfield, IA 52556
www.1stworldlibrary.com
First Edition

LCCN: 2006938081

Softcover ISBN: 978-1-4218-3377-4
Hardcover ISBN: 978-1-4218-3277-7
eBook ISBN: 978-1-4218-3477-1

Purchase *"The Turtles of Tasman"*
as a traditional bound book at:
www.1stWorldLibrary.com/purchase.asp?ISBN=978-1-4218-3377-4

1st World Library is a literary, educational organization
dedicated to:

- Creating a free internet library of downloadable ebooks

- Hosting writing competitions and offering book
publishing scholarships.

Interested in more 1st World Library books?
contact: literacy@1stworldlibrary.com
Check us out at: www.1stworldlibrary.com

1st World Library Literary Society

Giving Back to the World

"If you want to work on the core problem, it's early school literacy."

- James Barksdale, former CEO of Netscape

"No skill is more crucial to the future of a child, or to a democratic and prosperous society, than literacy."

- Los Angeles Times

Literacy... means far more than learning how to read and write... The aim is to transmit... knowledge and promote social participation."

- UNESCO

"Literacy is not a luxury, it is a right and a responsibility. If our world is to meet the challenges of the twenty-first century we must harness the energy and creativity of all our citizens."

- President Bill Clinton

"Parents should be encouraged to read to their children, and teachers should be equipped with all available techniques for teaching literacy, so the varying needs and capacities of individual kids can be taken into account."

- Hugh Mackay

TABLE OF CONTENTS

BY THE TURTLES OF TASMAN

I

Law, order, and restraint had carved Frederick Travers' face. It was the strong, firm face of one used to power and who had used power with wisdom and discretion. Clean living had made the healthy skin, and the lines graved in it were honest lines. Hard and devoted work had left its wholesome handiwork, that was all. Every feature of the man told the same story, from the clear blue of the eyes to the full head of hair, light brown, touched with grey, and smoothly parted and drawn straight across above the strong-domed forehead. He was a seriously groomed man, and the light summer business suit no more than befitted his alert years, while it did not shout aloud that its possessor was likewise the possessor of numerous millions of dollars and property.

For Frederick Travers hated ostentation. The machine that waited outside for him under the porte-cochere was sober black. It was the most expensive machine in the county, yet he did not care to flaunt its price or horse-power in a red flare across the landscape, which also was mostly his, from the sand dunes and the everlasting beat of the Pacific breakers, across the fat bottomlands and upland pastures, to the far summits clad with redwood forest and wreathed in fog and cloud.

A rustle of skirts caused him to look over his shoulder. Just the faintest hint of irritation showed in his manner. Not that his daughter was the object, however. Whatever it was, it seemed to lie on the desk before him.

"What is that outlandish name again?" she asked. "I know I shall never remember it. See, I've brought a pad to write it down."

Her voice was low and cool, and she was a tall, well-formed, clear-skinned young woman. In her voice and complacence she, too, showed the drill-marks of order and restraint.

Frederick Travers scanned the signature of one of two letters on the desk. "Bronislawa Plaskoweitzkaia Travers," he read; then spelled the difficult first portion, letter by letter, while his daughter wrote it down.

"Now, Mary," he added, "remember Tom was always harum scarum, and you must make allowances for this daughter of his. Her very name is—ah—disconcerting. I haven't seen him for years, and as for her...." A shrug epitomised his apprehension. He smiled with an effort at wit. "Just the same, they're as much your family as mine. If he *is* my brother, he is your uncle. And if she's my niece, you're both cousins."

Mary nodded. "Don't worry, father. I'll be nice to her, poor thing. What nationality was her mother?—to get such an awful name."

"I don't know. Russian, or Polish, or Spanish, or something. It was just like Tom. She was an actress or singer—I don't remember. They met in Buenos Ayres. It was an elopement. Her husband—"

"Then she was already married!"

Mary's dismay was unfeigned and spontaneous, and her father's irritation grew more pronounced. He had not meant that. It had slipped out.

"There was a divorce afterward, of course. I never knew the details. Her mother died out in China—no; in Tasmania. It was in China that Tom—" His lips shut with almost a snap. He was not going to make any more slips. Mary waited, then turned to the door, where she paused.

"I've given her the rooms over the rose court," she said. "And I'm going now to take a last look."

Frederick Travers turned back to the desk, as if to put the letters away, changed his mind, and slowly and ponderingly reread them.

"Dear Fred:

"It's been a long time since I was so near to the old home, and I'd like to take a run up. Unfortunately, I played ducks and drakes with my Yucatan project—I think I wrote about it—and I m broke as usual. Could you advance me funds for the run? I'd like to arrive first class. Polly is with me, you know. I wonder how you two will get along.

"Tom.

"P.S. If it doesn't bother you too much, send it along next mail."

"Dear Uncle Fred":

the other letter ran, in what seemed to him a strange, foreign-taught, yet distinctly feminine hand.

"Dad doesn't know I am writing this. He told me what he said to you. It is not true. He is coming home to die. He doesn't know it, but I've talked with the doctors. And he'll have to come home, for we have no money. We're in a stuffy little boarding house, and it is not the place for Dad. He's helped other persons all his life, and now is the time to help him. He didn't play ducks and drakes in Yucatan. I was with him, and I know. He dropped all he had there, and he was robbed. He can't play the business game against New Yorkers. That explains it all, and I am proud he can't.

"He always laughs and says I'll never be able to get along with you. But I don't agree with him. Besides, I've never seen a really, truly blood relative in my life, and there's your daughter. Think of it!—a real live cousin!

"In anticipation,
"Your niece,
"BRONISLAWA PLASKOWEITZKAIA TRAVERS.

"P.S. You'd better telegraph the money, or you won't see Dad at all. He doesn't know how sick he is, and if he meets any of his old friends he'll be off and away on some wild goose chase. He's beginning to talk Alaska. Says it will get the fever out of his bones. Please know that we must pay the boarding house, or else we'll arrive without luggage.

"B.P.T."

Frederick Travers opened the door of a large, built-in safe and methodically put the letters away in a compartment labelled "Thomas Travers."

"Poor Tom! Poor Tom!" he sighed aloud.

II

The big motor car waited at the station, and Frederick Travers thrilled as he always thrilled to the distant locomotive whistle of the train plunging down the valley of Isaac Travers River. First of all westering white-men, had Isaac Travers gazed on that splendid valley, its salmon-laden waters, its rich bottoms, and its virgin forest slopes. Having seen, he had grasped and never let go. "Land-poor," they had called him in the mid-settler period. But that had been in the days when the placers petered out, when there were no wagon roads nor tugs to draw in sailing vessels across the perilous bar, and when his lonely grist mill had been run under armed guards to keep the marauding Klamaths off while wheat was ground. Like father, like son, and what Isaac Travers had grasped, Frederick Travers had held. It had been the same tenacity of hold. Both had been far-visioned. Both had foreseen the transformation of the utter West, the coming of the railroad, and the building of the new empire on the Pacific shore.

Frederick Travers thrilled, too, at the locomotive whistle, because, more than any man's, it was his railroad. His father had died still striving to bring the railroad in across the mountains that averaged a hundred thousand dollars to the mile. He, Frederick, had brought it in. He had sat up nights over that railroad; bought newspapers, entered politics, and subsidised party machines; and he had made pilgrimages, more than once, at his own expense, to the railroad chiefs of the East. While all the county knew how many miles of his land were crossed by the right of way, none of the county guessed nor dreamed the number of his dollars which had gone into guaranties and railroad bonds. He had done much for his county, and the railroad was his last and greatest achievement, the capstone of the Travers' effort, the momentous and marvellous thing that had been brought about just yesterday. It had been running two years, and, highest proof of all of his judgment, dividends were in sight. And farther reaching reward was in sight. It was written in the books that the next

Governor of California was to be spelled, Frederick A. Travers.

Twenty years had passed since he had seen his elder brother, and then it had been after a gap of ten years. He remembered that night well. Tom was the only man who dared run the bar in the dark, and that last time, between nightfall and the dawn, with a southeaster breezing up, he had sailed his schooner in and out again. There had been no warning of his coming—a clatter of hoofs at midnight, a lathered horse in the stable, and Tom had appeared, the salt of the sea on his face as his mother attested. An hour only he remained, and on a fresh horse was gone, while rain squalls rattled upon the windows and the rising wind moaned through the redwoods, the memory of his visit a whiff, sharp and strong, from the wild outer world. A week later, sea-hammered and bar-bound for that time, had arrived the revenue cutter *Bear*, and there had been a column of conjecture in the local paper, hints of a heavy landing of opium and of a vain quest for the mysterious schooner *Halcyon*. Only Fred and his mother, and the several house Indians, knew of the stiffened horse in the barn and of the devious way it was afterward smuggled back to the fishing village on the beach.

Despite those twenty years, it was the same old Tom Travers that alighted from the Pullman. To his brother's eyes, he did not look sick. Older he was of course. The Panama hat did not hide the grey hair, and though indefinably hinting of shrunkenness, the broad shoulders were still broad and erect. As for the young woman with him, Frederick Travers experienced an immediate shock of distaste. He felt it vitally, yet vaguely. It was a challenge and a mock, yet he could not name nor place the source of it. It might have been the dress, of tailored linen and foreign cut, the shirtwaist, with its daring stripe, the black wilfulness of the hair, or the flaunt of poppies on the large straw hat or it might have been the flash and colour of her—the black eyes and brows, the flame of rose in the cheeks, the white of the even teeth that showed too readily. "A spoiled child," was his thought, but he had no time to analyse, for his brother's hand was in his and he was making his niece's acquaintance.

There it was again. She flashed and talked like her colour, and she talked with her hands as well. He could not avoid noting the smallness of them. They were absurdly small, and his eyes went to her feet to make the same discovery. Quite oblivious of the curious crowd on the station platform, she had intercepted his attempt to lead to the motor car and had ranged the brothers side by side. Tom had been laughingly acquiescent, but his younger brother was ill at ease, too conscious of the many eyes of his townspeople. He knew only the old Puritan way. Family displays were for the privacy of the family, not for the public. He was glad she had not attempted to kiss him. It was remarkable she had not. Already he apprehended anything of her.

She embraced them and penetrated them with sun-warm eyes that seemed to see through them, and over them, and all about them.

"You're really brothers," she cried, her hands flashing with her eyes. "Anybody can see it. And yet there is a difference—I don't know. I can't explain."

In truth, with a tact that exceeded Frederick Travers' farthest disciplined forbearance, she did not dare explain. Her wide artist-eyes had seen and sensed the whole trenchant and essential difference. Alike they looked, of the unmistakable same stock, their features reminiscent of a common origin; and there resemblance ceased. Tom was three inches taller, and well-greyed was the long, Viking moustache. His was the same eagle-like nose as his brother's, save that it was more eagle-like, while the blue eyes were pronouncedly so. The lines of the face were deeper, the cheek-bones higher, the hollows larger, the weather-beat darker. It was a volcanic face. There had been fire there, and the fire still lingered. Around the corners of the eyes were more laughter-wrinkles and in the eyes themselves a promise of deadlier seriousness than the younger brother possessed. Frederick was bourgeois in his carriage, but in

Tom's was a certain careless ease and distinction. It was the same pioneer blood of Isaac Travers in both men, but it had been retorted in widely different crucibles. Frederick represented the straight and expected line of descent. His brother expressed a vast and intangible something that was unknown in the Travers stock. And it was all this that the black-eyed girl saw and knew on the instant. All that had been inexplicable in the two men and their relationship cleared up in the moment she saw them side by side.

"Wake me up," Tom was saying. "I can't believe I arrived on a train. And the population? There were only four thousand thirty years ago."

"Sixty thousand now," was the other's answer. "And increasing by leaps and bounds. Want to spin around for a look at the city? There's plenty of time."

As they sped along the broad, well-paved streets, Tom persisted in his Rip Van Winkle pose. The waterfront perplexed him. Where he had once anchored his sloop in a dozen feet of water, he found solid land and railroad yards, with wharves and shipping still farther out.

"Hold on! Stop!" he cried, a few blocks on, looking up at a solid business block. "Where is this, Fred?"

"Fourth and Travers—don't you remember?"

Tom stood up and gazed around, trying to discern the anciently familiar configuration of the land under its clutter of buildings.

"I ... I think...." he began hesitantly. "No; by George, I'm sure of it. We used to hunt cottontails over that ground, and shoot blackbirds in the brush. And there, where the bank building is, was a pond." He turned to Polly. "I built my first raft there, and got my first taste of the sea."

"Heaven knows how many gallons of it," Frederick laughed, nodding to the chauffeur. "They rolled you on a barrel, I remember."

"Oh! More!" Polly cried, clapping her hands.

"There's the park," Frederick pointed out a little later, indicating a mass of virgin redwoods on the first dip of the bigger hills.

"Father shot three grizzlies there one afternoon," was Tom's remark.

"I presented forty acres of it to the city," Frederick went on. "Father bought the quarter section for a dollar an acre from Leroy."

Tom nodded, and the sparkle and flash in his eyes, like that of his daughter, were unlike anything that ever appeared in his brother's eyes.

"Yes," he affirmed, "Leroy, the negro squawman. I remember the time he carried you and me on his back to Alliance, the night the Indians burned the ranch. Father stayed behind and fought."

"But he couldn't save the grist mill. It was a serious setback to him."

"Just the same he nailed four Indians."

In Polly's eyes now appeared the flash and sparkle.

"An Indian-fighter!" she cried. "Tell me about him."

"Tell her about Travers Ferry," Tom said.

"That's a ferry on the Klamath River on the way to Orleans Bar and Siskiyou. There was great packing into the diggings in those days, and, among other things, father had made a location there. There was rich bench farming land, too. He built a suspension bridge—wove the cables on the spot with sailors and materials freighted in from the coast. It cost him twenty thousand dollars. The first day it was open, eight hundred mules crossed at a dollar a head, to say nothing of the toll for foot and horse. That night the river rose. The bridge was one hundred and forty feet above low water mark. Yet the freshet rose higher than that, and swept the bridge away. He'd have made a fortune there otherwise."

"That wasn't it at all," Tom blurted out impatiently. "It was at Travers Ferry that father and old Jacob Vance were caught by a war party of Mad River Indians. Old Jacob was killed right outside the door of the log cabin. Father dragged the body inside and stood the Indians off for a week. Father was some shot. He buried Jacob under the cabin floor."

"I still run the ferry," Frederick went on, "though there isn't so much travel as in the old days. I freight by wagon-road to the Reservation, and then mule-back on up the Klamath and clear in to the forks of Little Salmon. I have twelve stores on that chain now, a stage-line to the Reservation, and a hotel there. Quite a tourist trade is beginning to pick up."

And the girl, with curious brooding eyes, looked from brother to brother as they so differently voiced themselves and life.

"Ay, he was some man, father was," Tom murmured.

There was a drowsy note in his speech that drew a quick glance of anxiety from her. The machine had turned into the cemetery, and now halted before a substantial vault on the crest of the hill.

"I thought you'd like to see it," Frederick was saying. "I built that mausoleum myself, most of it with my own hands. Mother wanted it. The estate was dreadfully encumbered. The best bid I could get out of the contractors was eleven thousand.

I did it myself for a little over eight."

"Must have worked nights," Tom murmured admiringly and more sleepily than before.

"I did, Tom, I did. Many a night by lantern-light. I was so busy. I was reconstructing the water works then—the artesian wells had failed—and mother's eyes were troubling her. You remember—cataract—I wrote you. She was too weak to travel, and I brought the specialists up from San Francisco. Oh, my hands were full. I was just winding up the disastrous affairs of the steamer line father had established to San Francisco, and I was keeping up the interest on mortgages to the tune of one hundred and eighty thousand dollars."

A soft stertorous breathing interrupted him. Tom, chin on chest, was asleep. Polly, with a significant look, caught her uncle's eye. Then her father, after an uneasy restless movement, lifted drowsy lids.

"Deuced warm day," he said with a bright apologetic laugh. "I've been actually asleep. Aren't we near home?"

Frederick nodded to the chauffeur, and the car rolled on.

III

The house that Frederick Travers had built when his prosperity came, was large and costly, sober and comfortable, and with no more pretence than was naturally attendant on the finest country home in the county. Its atmosphere was just the sort that he and his daughter would create. But in the days that followed his brother's home-coming, all this was changed. Gone was the subdued and ordered repose. Frederick was neither comfortable nor happy. There was an unwonted flurry of life and violation of sanctions and traditions. Meals were irregular and protracted, and there were midnight chafing-dish suppers and bursts of laughter at the most inappropriate hours.

Frederick was abstemious. A glass of wine at dinner was his wildest excess. Three cigars a day he permitted himself, and these he smoked either on the broad veranda or in the smoking room. What else was a smoking room for? Cigarettes he detested. Yet his brother was ever rolling thin, brown-paper cigarettes and smoking them wherever he might happen to be. A litter of tobacco crumbs was always to be found in the big easy chair he frequented and among the cushions of the window-seats. Then there were the cocktails. Brought up under the stern tutelage of Isaac and Eliza Travers, Frederick looked upon liquor in the house as an abomination. Ancient cities had been smitten by God's wrath for just such practices. Before lunch and dinner, Tom, aided and abetted by Polly, mixed an endless variety of drinks, she being particularly adept with strange swivel-stick concoctions learned at the ends of the earth. To Frederick, at such times, it seemed that his butler's pantry and dining room had been turned into bar-rooms. When he suggested this, under a facetious show, Tom proclaimed that when he made his pile he would build a liquor cabinet in every living room of his house.

And there were more young men at the house than formerly, and they helped in disposing of the cocktails. Frederick would have liked to account in that manner for their presence, but he knew better. His brother and his brother's daughter did what he and Mary had failed to do. They were the magnets. Youth and joy and laughter drew to them. The house was lively with young life. Ever, day and night, the motor cars honked up and down the gravelled drives. There were picnics and expeditions in the summer weather, moonlight sails on the bay, starts before dawn or home-comings at midnight, and often, of nights, the many bedrooms were filled as they had never been before. Tom must cover all his boyhood ramblings, catch trout again on Bull Creek, shoot quail over Walcott's Prairie, get a deer on Round Mountain. That deer was a cause of pain and shame to Frederick. What if it was closed season? Tom had triumphantly brought home the buck and gleefully called it sidehill-salmon when it was served and eaten at Frederick's own table.

They had clambakes at the head of the bay and musselbakes down by the roaring surf; and Tom told shamelessly of the *Halcyon*, and of the run of contraband, and asked Frederick before them all how he had managed to smuggle the horse back to the fishermen without discovery. All the young men were in the conspiracy with Polly to pamper Tom to his heart's desire. And Frederick heard the true inwardness of the killing of the deer; of its purchase from the overstocked Golden Gate Park; of its crated carriage by train, horse-team and mule-back to the fastnesses of Round Mountain; of Tom falling asleep beside the deer-run the first time it was driven by; of the pursuit by the young men, the jaded saddle horses, the scrambles and the falls, and the roping of it at Burnt Ranch Clearing; and, finally, of the triumphant culmination, when it was driven past a second time and Tom had dropped it at fifty yards. To Frederick there was a vague hurt in it all. When had such consideration been shown him?

There were days when Tom could not go out, postponements of outdoor frolics, when, still the centre, he sat and drowsed in the big chair, waking, at times, in that unexpected queer, bright way of his, to roll a cigarette and call for his *ukulele*—a sort of miniature guitar of Portuguese invention. Then, with strumming and tumtuming, the live cigarette laid aside to the imminent peril of polished wood, his full baritone would roll out in South Sea *hulas* and sprightly French and Spanish songs.

One, in particular, had pleased Frederick at first. The favourite song of a Tahitian king, Tom explained—the last of the Pomares, who had himself composed it and was wont to lie on his mats by the hour singing it. It consisted of the repetition of a few syllables. "*E meu ru ru a vau,*" it ran, and that was all of it, sung in a stately, endless, ever-varying chant, accompanied by solemn chords from the *ukelele*. Polly took great joy in teaching it to her uncle, but when, himself questing for some of this genial flood of life that bathed about his brother, Frederick essayed the song, he noted suppressed glee on the part of his listeners, which increased, through giggles and snickers, to a great outburst of laughter. To his disgust and dismay, he learned that the simple phrase he had repeated and repeated was nothing else than "I am so drunk." He had been made a fool of. Over and over, solemnly and gloriously, he, Frederick Travers, had announced how drunk he was. After that, he slipped quietly out of the room whenever it was sung. Nor could Polly's later explanation that the last word was "happy," and not "drunk," reconcile him; for she had been compelled to admit that the old king was a toper, and that he was always in his cups when he struck up the chant.

Frederick was constantly oppressed by the feeling of being out of it all. He was a social being, and he liked fun, even if it were of a more wholesome and dignified brand than that to which his brother was addicted. He could not understand why in the past the young people had voted his house a bore and come no more, save on state and formal occasions, until now, when they flocked to it and to his brother, but not to him. Nor could he like the way the young women petted his brother, and called him Tom, while it was intolerable to see them twist and pull his buccaneer moustache in mock punishment when his sometimes too-jolly banter sank home to them.

Such conduct was a profanation to the memory of Isaac and Eliza Travers. There was too much an air of revelry in the house. The long table was never shortened, while there was extra help in the kitchen. Breakfast extended from four until eleven, and the midnight suppers, entailing raids on the pantry and complaints from the servants, were a vexation to Frederick. The house had become a restaurant, a hotel, he sneered bitterly to himself; and there were times when he was sorely tempted to put his foot down and reassert the old ways. But somehow the ancient sorcery of his masterful brother was too strong upon him; and at times he gazed upon him with a sense almost of awe, groping to fathom the alchemy of charm, baffled by the strange lights and fires in his brother's eyes, and by the wisdom of far places and of wild nights and days written in his face. What was it? What lordly vision had the other glimpsed?—he, the irresponsible and careless one? Frederick remembered a line of an old song—"Along the shining ways he came." Why did his brother remind him of that line? Had he, who in boyhood had known no law, who in manhood had exalted himself above law, in truth found the shining ways?

There was an unfairness about it that perplexed Frederick, until he found solace in dwelling upon the failure Tom had made of life Then it was, in quiet intervals, that he got some comfort and stiffened his own pride by showing Tom over the estate.

"You have done well, Fred," Tom would say. "You have done very well."

He said it often, and often he drowsed in the big smooth-running machine.

"Everything orderly and sanitary and spick and span—not a blade of grass out of place," was Polly's comment. "How do you ever manage it? I should not like to be a blade of grass on your land," she concluded, with a little shivery shudder.

"You have worked hard," Tom said.

"Yes, I have worked hard," Frederick affirmed. "It was worth it."

He was going to say more, but the strange flash in the girl's eyes brought him to an uncomfortable pause. He felt that she measured him, challenged him. For the first time his honourable career of building a county commonwealth had been questioned—and by a chit of a girl, the daughter of a wastrel, herself but a flighty, fly-away, foreign creature.

Conflict between them was inevitable. He had disliked her from the first moment of meeting. She did not have to speak. Her mere presence made him uncomfortable. He felt her unspoken disapproval, though there were times when she did not stop at that. Nor did she mince language. She spoke forthright, like a man, and as no man had ever dared to speak to him.

"I wonder if you ever miss what you've missed," she told him. "Did you ever, once in your life, turn yourself loose and rip things up by the roots? Did you ever once get drunk? Or smoke yourself black in the face? Or dance a hoe-down on the ten commandments? Or stand up on your hind legs and wink like a good fellow at God?"

"Isn't she a rare one!" Tom gurgled. "Her mother over again."

Outwardly smiling and calm, there was a chill of horror at Frederick's heart. It was incredible.

"I think it is the English," she continued, "who have a saying that a man has not lived until he has kissed his woman and struck his man. I wonder—confess up, now—if you ever struck a man."

"Have you?" he countered.

She nodded, an angry reminiscent flash in her eyes, and waited.

"No, I have never had that pleasure," he answered slowly. "I early learned control."

Later, irritated by his self-satisfied complacence and after listening to a recital of how he had cornered the Klamath salmon-packing, planted the first oysters on the bay and established that lucrative monopoly, and of how, after exhausting litigation and a campaign of years he had captured the water front of Williamsport and thereby won to control of the Lumber Combine, she returned to the charge.

"You seem to value life in terms of profit and loss," she said. "I wonder if you have ever known love."

The shaft went home. He had not kissed his woman. His marriage had been one of policy. It had saved the estate in the days when he had been almost beaten in the struggle to disencumber the vast holdings Isaac Travers' wide hands had grasped. The girl was a witch. She had probed an old wound and made it hurt again. He had never had time to love. He had worked hard. He had been president of the chamber of commerce, mayor of the city, state senator, but he had missed love. At chance moments he had come upon Polly, openly and shamelessly in her father's arms, and he had noted the warmth and tenderness in their eyes. Again he knew that he had missed love. Wanton as was the display, not even in private did he and Mary so behave. Normal, formal, and colourless, she was what was to be expected of a loveless marriage. He even puzzled to decide whether the feeling he felt for her was love. Was he himself loveless as well?

In the moment following Polly's remark, he was aware of a great emptiness. It seemed that his hands had grasped ashes, until, glancing into the other room, he saw Tom asleep in the big chair, very grey and aged and tired. He remembered all that he had done, all that he possessed. Well, what did Tom possess? What had Tom done?—save play ducks and drakes with life and wear it out until all that remained was that dimly flickering spark in a dying body.

What bothered Frederick in Polly was that she attracted him as well as repelled him. His own daughter had never interested him in that way. Mary moved along frictionless grooves, and to forecast her actions was so effortless that it was automatic. But Polly! many-hued, protean-natured, he never knew what she was going to do next.

"Keeps you guessing, eh?" Tom chuckled.

She was irresistible. She had her way with Frederick in ways that in Mary would have been impossible. She took liberties with him, cosened him or hurt him, and compelled always in him a sharp awareness of her existence.

Once, after one of their clashes, she devilled him at the piano, playing a mad damned thing that stirred and irritated him and set his pulse pounding wild and undisciplined fancies in the ordered chamber of his brain. The worst of it was she saw and knew just what she was doing. She was aware before he was, and she made him aware, her face turned to look at him, on her lips a mocking, contemplative smile that was almost a superior sneer. It was this that shocked him into consciousness of the orgy his imagination had been playing him. From the wall above her, the stiff portraits of Isaac and Eliza Travers looked down like reproachful spectres. Infuriated, he left the room. He had never dreamed such potencies resided in music. And then, and he remembered it with shame, he had stolen back outside to listen, and she had known, and once more she had devilled him.

When Mary asked him what he thought of Polly's playing, an unbidden contrast leaped to his mind. Mary's music reminded him of church. It was cold and bare as a Methodist meeting house. But Polly's was like the mad and lawless ceremonial of some heathen temple where incense arose and nautch girls writhed.

"She plays like a foreigner," he answered, pleased with the success and oppositeness of his evasion.

"She is an artist," Mary affirmed solemnly. "She is a genius. When does she ever practise? When did she ever practise? You know how I have. My best is like a five-finger exercise compared with the foolishest thing she ripples off. Her music tells me things—oh, things wonderful and unutterable. Mine tells me, 'one-two-three, one-two-three.' Oh, it is maddening! I work and work and get nowhere. It is unfair. Why should she be born that way, and not I?"

"Love," was Frederick's immediate and secret thought; but before he could dwell upon the conclusion, the unprecedented had happened and Mary was sobbing in a break-down of tears. He would have liked to take her in his arms, after Tom's fashion, but he did not know how. He tried, and found Mary as unschooled as himself. It resulted only in an embarrassed awkwardness for both of them.

The contrasting of the two girls was inevitable. Like father like daughter. Mary was no more than a pale camp-follower of a gorgeous, conquering general. Frederick's thrift had been sorely educated in the matter of clothes. He knew just how expensive Mary's clothes were, yet he could not blind himself to the fact that Polly's vagabond makeshifts, cheap and apparently haphazard, were always all right and far more successful. Her taste was unerring. Her ways with a shawl were inimitable. With a scarf she performed miracles.

"She just throws things together," Mary complained. "She doesn't even try. She can dress in fifteen minutes, and when she goes swimming she beats the boys out of the dressing rooms." Mary was honest and incredulous in her admiration. "I can't see how she does it. No one could dare those colours, but they look just right on her."

"She's always threatened that when I became finally flat broke she'd set up dressmaking and take care of both of us," Tom contributed.

Frederick, looking over the top of a newspaper, was witness to an illuminating scene; Mary, to his certain knowledge, had been primping for an hour ere she appeared.

"Oh! How lovely!" was Polly's ready appreciation. Her eyes and face glowed with honest pleasure, and her hands wove their delight in the air. "But why not wear that bow so and thus?"

Her hands flashed to the task, and in a moment the miracle of taste and difference achieved by her touch was apparent even to Frederick.

Polly was like her father, generous to the point of absurdity with her meagre possessions. Mary admired a Spanish fan—a Mexican treasure that had come down from one of the grand ladies of the Court of the Emperor Maximilian. Polly's delight flamed like wild-fire. Mary found herself the immediate owner of the fan, almost labouring under the fictitious impression that she had conferred an obligation by accepting it. Only a foreign woman could do such things, and Polly was guilty of similar gifts to all the young women. It was her way. It might be a lace handkerchief, a pink Paumotan pearl, or a comb of hawksbill turtle. It was all the same. Whatever their eyes rested on in joy was theirs. To women, as to men, she was irresistible.

"I don't dare admire anything any more," was Mary's plaint. "If I do she always gives it to me."

Frederick had never dreamed such a creature could exist. The women of his own race and place had never adumbrated such a possibility. He knew that whatever she did—her quick generosities, her hot enthusiasms or angers, her birdlike caressing ways—was unbelievably sincere. Her extravagant moods at the same time shocked and fascinated him. Her voice was as mercurial as her feelings. There were no even tones, and she talked with her hands. Yet, in her mouth, English was a new and beautiful language, softly limpid, with an audacity of phrase and tellingness of expression that conveyed subtleties and nuances as unambiguous and direct as they were unexpected from one of such childlikeness and simplicity. He woke up of nights and on his darkened eyelids saw bright memory-pictures of the backward turn of her vivid, laughing face.

Like daughter like father. Tom, too, had been irresistible. All the world still called to him, and strange men came from time to time with its messages. Never had there been such visitors to the Travers home. Some came with the reminiscent roll of the sea in their gait. Others were black-browed ruffians; still others were fever-burnt and sallow; and about all of them was something bizarre and outlandish. Their talk was likewise bizarre and outlandish, of things to Frederick unguessed and undreamed, though he recognised the men for what they were—soldiers of fortune, adventurers, free lances of the world. But the big patent thing was the love and loyalty they bore their leader. They named him variously?—Black Tom, Blondine, Husky Travers, Malemute Tom, Swiftwater Tom— but most of all he was Captain Tom. Their projects and propositions were equally various, from the South Sea trader with the discovery of a new guano island and the Latin-American with a nascent revolution on his hands, on through Siberian gold chases and the prospecting of the placer benches of the upper Kuskokeem, to darker things that were mentioned only in whispers. And Captain Tom regretted the temporary indisposition that prevented immediate departure with them, and continued to sit and drowse more and more in the big chair. It was Polly, with a camaraderie distasteful to her uncle, who got these men aside and broke the news that Captain Tom would never go out on the shining ways again. But not all of them came with projects. Many made love-calls on their leader of old and unforgetable days, and Frederick sometimes was a witness to their meeting, and he marvelled anew at the mysterious charm in his brother that drew all men to him.

"By the turtles of Tasman!" cried one, "when I heard you was in California, Captain Tom, I just had to come and shake hands. I reckon you ain't forgot Tasman, eh?—nor the scrap at Thursday Island. Say—old Tasman was killed by his niggers only last year up German New Guinea way. Remember his cook-boy?—Ngani-Ngani? He was the ringleader. Tasman swore by him, but Ngani-Ngani hatcheted him just the same."

"Shake hands with Captain Carlsen, Fred," was Tom's introduction of his brother to another visitor. "He pulled me out of a tight place on the West Coast once. I'd have cashed in, Carlsen, if you hadn't happened along."

Captain Carlsen was a giant hulk of a man, with gimlet eyes of palest blue, a slash-scarred mouth that a blazing red beard could not quite hide, and a grip in his hand that made Frederick squirm.

A few minutes later, Tom had his brother aside.

"Say, Fred, do you think it will bother to advance me a thousand?"

"Of course," Frederick answered splendidly. "You know half of that I have is yours, Tom."

And when Captain Carlsen departed, Frederick was morally certain that the thousand dollars departed with him.

Small wonder Tom had made a failure of life—and come home to die. Frederick sat at his own orderly desk taking stock of the difference between him and his brother. Yes, and if it hadn't been for him, there would have been no home for Tom to die in.

Frederick cast back for solace through their joint history. It was he who had always been the mainstay, the dependable one. Tom had laughed and rollicked, played hooky from school, disobeyed Isaac's commandments. To the mountains or the sea, or in hot water with the neighbours and the town authorities—it was all the same; he was everywhere save where the dull plod of work obtained. And work was work in those backwoods days, and he, Frederick, had done the work. Early and late and all days he had been at it. He remembered the season when Isaac's wide plans had taken one of their smashes, when food had been scarce on the table of a man who owned a hundred thousand acres, when there had been no money to hire harvesters for the hay, and when Isaac would not let go his grip on a single one of his acres. He, Frederick, had pitched the hay, while Isaac mowed and raked. Tom had lain in bed and run up a doctor bill with a broken leg, gained by falling off the ridge-pole of the barn—which place was the last in the world to which any one would expect to go to pitch hay. About the only work Tom had ever done, it seemed to him, was to fetch in venison and bear-oil, to break colts, and to raise a din in the valley pastures and wooded canyons with his bear-hounds.

Tom was the elder, yet when Isaac died, the estate, with all its vast possibilities would have gone to ruin, had not he, Frederick, buckled down to it and put the burden on his back. Work! He remembered the enlargement of the town water-system—how he had manoeuvred and financed, persuaded small loans at ruinous interest, and laid pipe and made joints by lantern light while the workmen slept, and then been up ahead of them to outline and direct and rack his brains over the raising of the next week-end wages. For he had carried on old Isaac's policy. He would not let go. The future would vindicate.

And Tom!—with a bigger pack of bear dogs ranging the mountains and sleeping out a week at a time. Frederick remembered the final conference in the kitchen—Tom, and he, and Eliza Travers, who still cooked and baked and washed dishes on an estate that carried a hundred and eighty thousand dollars in mortgages.

"Don't divide," Eliza Travers had pleaded, resting her soap-flecked, parboiled arms. "Isaac was right. It will be worth millions. The country is opening up. We must all pull together."

"I don't want the estate," Tom cried. "Let Frederick have it. What I want...."

He never completed the sentence, but all the vision of the world burned in his eyes.

"I can't wait," he went on. "You can have the millions when they come. In the meantime let me have ten thousand. I'll sign off quitclaim to everything. And give me the old schooner, and some day I'll be back with a pot of money to help you out."

Frederick could see himself, in that far past day, throwing up his arms in horror and crying:

"Ten thousand!—when I'm strained to the breaking point to raise this quarter's interest!"

"There's the block of land next to the court house," Tom had urged. "I know the bank has a standing offer for ten thousand."

"But it will be worth a hundred thousand in ten years," Frederick had objected.

"Call it so. Say I quitclaim everything for a hundred thousand. Sell it for ten and let me have it. It's all I want, and I want it now. You can have the rest."

And Tom had had his will as usual (the block had been mortgaged instead of sold), and sailed away in the old schooner, the benediction of the town upon his head, for he had carried away in his crew half the riff-raff of the beach.

The bones of the schooner had been left on the coast of Java. That had been when Eliza Travers was being operated on for her eyes, and Frederick had kept it from her until indubitable proof came that Tom was still alive.

Frederick went over to his files and drew out a drawer labelled "Thomas Travers." In it were packets, methodically arranged. He went over the letters. They were from everywhere—China, Rangoon, Australia, South Africa, the Gold Coast, Patagonia,

Armenia, Alaska. Briefly and infrequently written, they epitomised the wanderer's life. Frederick ran over in his mind a few of the glimpsed highlights of Tom's career. He had fought in some sort of foreign troubles in Armenia. He had been an officer in the Chinese army, and it was a certainty that the trade he later drove in the China Seas was illicit. He had been caught running arms into Cuba. It seemed he had always been running something somewhere that it ought not to have been run. And he had never outgrown it. One letter, on crinkly tissue paper, showed that as late as the Japanese-Russian War he had been caught running coal into Port Arthur and been taken to the prize court at Sasebo, where his steamer was confiscated and he remained a prisoner until the end of the war.

Frederick smiled as he read a paragraph: "*How do you prosper? Let me know any time a few thousands will help you.*" He looked at the date, April 18, 1883, and opened another packet. "*May 5th,*" 1883, was the dated sheet he drew out. "*Five thousand will put me on my feet again. If you can, and love me, send it along pronto—that's Spanish for rush.*"

He glanced again at the two dates. It was evident that somewhere between April 18th and May 5th Tom had come a cropper. With a smile, half bitter, Frederick skimmed on through the correspondence: "*There's a wreck on Midway Island. A fortune in it, salvage you know. Auction in two days. Cable me four thousand.*" The last he examined, ran: "*A deal I can swing with a little cash. It's big, I tell you. It's so big I don't dare tell you.*" He remembered that deal—a Latin-American revolution. He had sent the cash, and Tom had swung it, and himself as well, into a prison cell and a death sentence.

Tom had meant well, there was no denying that. And he had always religiously forwarded his I O U's. Frederick musingly weighed the packet of them in his hand, as though to determine if any relation existed between the weight of paper and the sums of money represented on it.

He put the drawer back in the cabinet and passed out. Glancing in at the big chair he saw Polly just tiptoeing from the room. Tom's head lay back, and his breathing was softly heavy, the sickness pronouncedly apparent on his relaxed face.

V

"I have worked hard," Frederick explained to Polly that evening on the veranda, unaware that when a man explains it is a sign his situation is growing parlous. "I have done what came to my hand—how creditably it is for others to say. And I have been paid for it. I have taken care of others and taken care of myself. The doctors say they have never seen such a constitution in a man of my years. Why, almost half my life is yet before me, and we Travers are a long-lived stock. I took care of myself, you see, and I have myself to show for it. I was not a waster. I conserved my heart and my arteries, and yet there are few men who can boast having done as much work as I have done. Look at that hand. Steady, eh? It will be as steady twenty years from now. There is nothing in playing fast and loose with oneself."

And all the while Polly had been following the invidious comparison that lurked behind his words.

"You can write 'Honourable' before your name," she flashed up proudly. "But my father has been a king. He has lived. Have you lived? What have you got to show for it? Stocks and bonds, and houses and servants—pouf! Heart and arteries and a steady hand—is that all? Have you lived merely to live? Were you afraid to die? I'd rather sing one wild song and burst my heart with it, than live a thousand years watching my digestion and being afraid of the wet. When you are dust, my father will be ashes. That is the difference."

"But my dear child—" he began.

"What have you got to show for it?" she flamed on. "Listen!"

From within, through the open window, came the tinkling of Tom's *ukulele* and the rollicking lilt of his voice in an Hawaiian *hula*. It ended in a throbbing, primitive love-call from the sensuous tropic night that no one could mistake.

There was a burst of young voices, and a clamour for more. Frederick did not speak. He had sensed something vague and significant.

Turning, he glanced through the window at Tom, flushed and royal, surrounded by the young men and women, under his Viking moustache lighting a cigarette from a match held to him by one of the girls. It abruptly struck Frederick that never had he lighted a cigar at a match held in a woman's hand.

"Doctor Tyler says he oughtn't to smoke—it only aggravates," he said; and it was all he could say.

As the fall of the year came on, a new type of men began to frequent the house. They proudly called themselves "sourdoughs," and they were arriving in San Francisco on the winter's furlough from the gold-diggings of Alaska. More and more of them came, and they pre-empted a large portion of one of the down-town hotels. Captain Tom was fading with the season, and almost lived in the big chair. He drowsed oftener and longer, but whenever he awoke he was surrounded by his court of young people, or there was some comrade waiting to sit and yarn about the old gold days and plan for the new gold days.

For Tom—Husky Travers, the Yukoners named him—never thought that the end approached. A temporary illness, he called it, the natural enfeeblement following upon a prolonged bout with Yucatan fever. In the spring he would be right and fit again. Cold weather was what he needed. His blood had been cooked. In the meantime it was a case of take it easy and make the most of the rest.

And no one undeceived him—not even the Yukoners, who smoked pipes and black cigars and chewed tobacco on Frederick's broad verandas until he felt like an intruder in his own house. There was no touch with them. They regarded him as a stranger to be tolerated. They came to see Tom. And their manner of seeing him was provocative of innocent envy pangs to Frederick. Day after day he watched them. He would see the Yukoners meet, perhaps one just leaving the sick room and one just going in. They would clasp hands, solemnly and silently, outside the door. The newcomer would question with his eyes, and the other would shake his head. And more than once Frederick noted the moisture in their eyes. Then the newcomer would enter and draw his chair up to Tom's, and with jovial voice proceed to plan the outfitting for the exploration of the upper Kuskokeem; for it was there Tom was bound in the spring. Dogs could be had at Larabee's—a clean breed, too, with no taint of the soft Southland strains. It was rough country, it was reported, but if sour-doughs couldn't make the traverse from Larabee's in forty days they'd like to see a *chechako* do it in sixty.

And so it went, until Frederick wondered, when he came to die, if there was one man in the county, much less in the adjoining county, who would come to him at his bedside.

Seated at his desk, through the open windows would drift whiffs of strong tobacco and rumbling voices, and he could not help catching snatches of what the Yukoners talked.

"D'ye recollect that Koyokuk rush in the early nineties?" he would hear one say. "Well, him an' me was pardners then, tradin' an' such. We had a dinky little steamboat, the *Blatterbat*. He named her that, an' it stuck. He was a caution. Well, sir, as I was sayin', him an' me loaded the little *Blatterbat* to the guards an' started up the Koyokuk, me firin' an' engineerin' an' him steerin', an' both of us deck-handin'. Once in a while we'd tie to the bank an' cut firewood. It was the fall, an' mush-ice was comin' down, an' everything gettin' ready for the freeze up. You see, we was north of the Arctic Circle then an' still headin' north. But they was two hundred miners in there needin' grub if they wintered, an' we had the grub.

"Well, sir, pretty soon they begun to pass us, driftin' down the river in canoes an' rafts. They was pullin' out. We kept track of them. When a hundred an' ninety-four had passed, we didn't see no reason for keepin' on. So we turned tail and started down. A cold snap had come, an' the water was fallin' fast, an' dang me if we didn't ground on a bar—up-stream side. The *Blatterbat* hung up solid. Couldn't budge her. 'It's a shame to waste all that grub,' says I, just as we was pullin' out in a canoe. 'Let's stay an' eat it,' says he. An' dang me if we didn't. We wintered right there on the *Blatterbat*, huntin' and tradin' with the Indians, an' when the river broke next year we brung down eight thousand dollars' worth of skins. Now a whole winter, just two of us, is goin' some. But never a cross word out of him. Best-tempered pardner I ever seen. But fight!"

"Huh!" came the other voice. "I remember the winter Oily Jones allowed he'd clean out Forty Mile. Only he didn't, for about the second yap he let off he ran afoul of Husky Travers. It was in the White Caribou. 'I'm a wolf!' yaps Jones. You know his style, a gun in his belt, fringes on his moccasins, and long hair down his back. 'I'm a wolf,' he yaps, 'an' this is my night to howl. Hear me, you long lean makeshift of a human critter?'—an' this to Husky Travers."

"Well?" the other voice queried, after a pause.

"In about a second an' a half Oily Jones was on the floor an' Husky on top askin' somebody kindly to pass him a butcher knife. What's he do but plumb hack off all of Oily Jones' long hair. 'Now howl, damn you, howl,' says Husky, gettin' up."

"He was a cool one, for a wild one," the first voice took up. "I seen him buck roulette in the Little Wolverine, drop nine thousand in two hours, borrow some more, win it back in fifteen minutes, buy the drinks, an' cash in—dang me, all in fifteen minutes."

One evening Tom was unusually brightly awake, and Frederick, joining the rapt young circle, sat and listened to his brother's serio-comic narrative of the night of wreck on the island of Blarg; of the swim through the sharks where half the crew was lost; of the great pearl which Desay brought ashore with him; of the head-decorated palisade that surrounded the grass palace wherein dwelt the Malay queen with her royal consort, a shipwrecked Chinese Eurasian; of the intrigue for the pearl of Desay; of mad feasts and dances in the barbaric night, and quick dangers and sudden deaths; of the queen's love-making to Desay, of Desay's love-making to the queen's daughter, and of Desay, every joint crushed, still alive, staked out on the reef at low tide to be eaten by the sharks; of the coming of the plague; of the beating of tom-toms and the exorcising of the devil-devil doctors; of the flight over the man-trapped, wild-pig runs of the mountain bush-men; and of the final rescue by Tasman, he who was hatcheted only last year and whose head reposed in some Melanesian stronghold—and all breathing of the warmth and abandon and savagery of the burning islands of the sun.

And despite himself, Frederick sat entranced; and when all the tale was told, he was aware of a queer emptiness. He remembered back to his boyhood, when he had pored over the illustrations in the old-fashioned geography. He, too, had dreamed of amazing adventure in far places and desired to go out on the shining ways. And he had planned to go; yet he had known only work and duty. Perhaps that was the difference. Perhaps that was the secret of the strange wisdom in his brother's eyes. For the moment, faint and far, vicariously, he glimpsed the lordly vision his brother had seen. He remembered a sharp saying of Polly's. "You have missed romance. You traded it for dividends." She was right, and yet, not fair. He had wanted romance, but the work had been placed ready to his hand. He had toiled and moiled, day and night, and been faithful to his trust. Yet he had missed love and the world-living that was forever a-whisper in his brother. And what had Tom done to deserve it?—a wastrel and an idle singer of songs.

His place was high. He was going to be the next governor of California. But what man would come to him and lie to him out of love? The thought of all his property seemed to put a dry and gritty taste in his mouth. Property! Now that he looked at it, one thousand dollars was like any other thousand dollars; and one day (of his days) was like any other day. He had never made the pictures in the geography come true. He had not struck his man, nor lighted his cigar at a match held in a woman's hand. A man could sleep in only one bed at a time—Tom had said that. He shuddered as he strove to estimate how many beds he owned, how many blankets he had bought. And all the beds and blankets would not buy one man to come from the end of the earth, and grip his hand, and cry, "By the turtles of Tasman!"

Something of all this he told Polly, an undercurrent of complaint at the unfairness of things in his tale. And she had answered:

"It couldn't have been otherwise. Father bought it. He never drove bargains. It was a royal thing, and he paid for it royally. You grudged the price, don't you see. You saved your arteries and your money and kept your feet dry."

VI

On an afternoon in the late fall all were gathered about the big chair and Captain Tom. Though he did not know it, he had drowsed the whole day through and only just awakened to call for his *ukulele* and light a cigarette at Polly's hand. But the *ukulele* lay idle on his arm, and though the pine logs crackled in the huge fireplace he shivered and took note of the cold.

"It's a good sign," he said, unaware that the faintness of his voice drew the heads of his listeners closer. "The cold weather will be a tonic. It's a hard job to work the tropics out of one's blood. But I'm beginning to shape up now for the Kuskokeem. In the spring, Polly, we start with the dogs, and you'll see the midnight sun. How your mother would have liked the trip. She was a game one. Forty sleeps with the dogs, and we'll be shaking out yellow nuggets from the moss-roots. Larabee has some fine animals. I know the breed. They're timber wolves, that's what they are, big grey timber wolves, though they sport brown about one in a litter—isn't that right, Bennington?"

"One in a litter, that's just about the average," Bennington, the Yukoner, replied promptly, but in a voice hoarsely unrecognisable.

"And you must never travel alone with them," Captain Tom went on. "For if you fall down they'll jump you. Larabee's brutes only respect a man when he stands upright on his legs. When he goes down, he's meat. I remember coming over the divide from Tanana to Circle City. That was before the Klondike strike. It was in '94 ... no, '95, and the bottom had dropped out of the thermometer. There was a young Canadian with the outfit. His name was it was ... a peculiar one ... wait a minute it will come to me...."

His voice ceased utterly, though his lips still moved. A look of unbelief and vast surprise dawned on his face. Followed a sharp, convulsive shudder. And in that moment, without warning, he saw Death. He looked clear-eyed and steady, as if pondering, then turned to Polly. His hand moved impotently, as if to reach hers, and when he found it, his fingers could not close. He gazed at her with a great smile that slowly faded. The eyes drooped as the life went out, and remained a face of quietude and repose. The *ukulele* clattered to the floor. One by one they went softly from the room, leaving Polly alone.

From the veranda, Frederick watched a man coming up the driveway. By the roll of the sea in his walk, Frederick could guess for whom the stranger came. The face was swarthy with sun and wrinkled with age that was given the lie by the briskness of his movements and the alertness in the keen black eyes. In the lobe of each ear was a tiny circlet of gold.

"How do you do, sir," the man said, and it was patent that English was not the tongue he had learned at his mother's knee. "How's Captain Tom? They told me in the town that he was sick."

"My brother is dead," Frederick answered.

The stranger turned his head and gazed out over the park-like grounds and up to the distant redwood peaks, and Frederick noted that he swallowed with an effort.

"By the turtles of Tasman, he was a man," he said, in a deep, changed voice.

"By the turtles of Tasman, he was a man," Frederick repeated; nor did he stumble over the unaccustomed oath.

THE ETERNITY OF FORMS

A strange life has come to an end in the death of Mr. Sedley Crayden, of Crayden Hill.

Mild, harmless, he was the victim of a strange delusion that kept him pinned, night and day, in his chair for the last two years of his life. The mysterious death, or, rather, disappearance, of his elder brother, James Crayden, seems to have preyed upon his mind, for it was shortly after that event that his delusion began to manifest itself.

Mr. Crayden never vouchsafed any explanation of his strange conduct. There was nothing the matter with him physically; and, mentally, the alienists found him normal in every way save for his one remarkable idiosyncrasy. His remaining in his chair was purely voluntary, an act of his own will. And now he is dead, and the mystery remains unsolved.

—*Extract from the Newton Courier-Times.*

Briefly, I was Mr. Sedley Crayden's confidential servant and valet for the last eight months of his life. During that time he wrote a great deal in a manuscript that he kept always beside him, except when he drowsed or slept, at which times he invariably locked it in a desk drawer close to his hand.

I was curious to read what the old gentleman wrote, but he was too cautious and cunning. I never got a peep at the manuscript. If he were engaged upon it when I attended on him, he covered the top sheet with a large blotter. It was I who found him dead in his chair, and it was then that I took the liberty of abstracting the manuscript. I was very curious to read it, and I have no excuses to offer.

After retaining it in my secret possession for several years, and after ascertaining that Mr. Crayden left no surviving relatives, I have decided to make the nature of the manuscript known. It is very long, and I have omitted nearly all of it, giving only the more lucid fragments. It bears all the earmarks of a disordered mind, and various experiences are repeated over and over, while much is so vague and incoherent as to defy comprehension. Nevertheless, from reading it myself, I venture to predict that if an excavation is made in the main basement, somewhere in the vicinity of the foundation of the great chimney, a collection of bones will be found which should very closely resemble those which James Crayden once clothed in mortal flesh.

—Statement of Rudolph Heckler.

Here follows the excerpts from the manuscript, made and arranged by Rudolph Heckler:

I never killed my brother. Let this be my first word and my last. Why should I kill him? We lived together in unbroken harmony for twenty years. We were old men, and the fires and tempers of youth had long since burned out. We never disagreed even over the most trivial things. Never was there such amity as ours. We were scholars. We cared nothing for the outside world. Our companionship and our books were all-satisfying. Never were there such talks as we held. Many a night we have sat up till two and three in the morning, conversing, weighing opinions and judgments, referring to authorities—in short, we lived at high and friendly intellectual altitudes.

*   *   *   *   *

He disappeared. I suffered a great shock. Why should he have disappeared? Where could he have gone? It was very strange. I was stunned. They say I was very sick for weeks. It was brain fever. This was caused by his inexplicable disappearance. It was at the beginning of the experience I hope here to relate, that he disappeared.

How I have endeavoured to find him. I am not an excessively rich man, yet have I offered continually increasing rewards. I have advertised in all the papers, and sought the aid of all the detective bureaus. At the present moment, the rewards I have out aggregate over fifty thousand dollars.

* * * * *

They say he was murdered. They also say murder will out. Then I say, why does not his murder come out? Who did it? Where is he? Where is Jim? My Jim?

* * * * *

We were so happy together. He had a remarkable mind, a most remarkable mind, so firmly founded, so widely informed, so rigidly logical, that it was not at all strange that we agreed in all things. Dissension was unknown between us. Jim was the most truthful man I have ever met. In this, too, we were similar, as we were similar in our intellectual honesty. We never sacrificed truth to make a point. We had no points to make, we so thoroughly agreed. It is absurd to think that we could disagree on anything under the sun.

* * * * *

I wish he would come back. Why did he go? Who can ever explain it? I am lonely now, and depressed with grave forebodings—frightened by terrors that are of the mind and that put at naught all that my mind has ever conceived. Form is mutable. This is the last word of positive science. The dead do not come back. This is incontrovertible. The dead are dead, and that is the end of it, and of them. And yet I have had experiences here—here, in this very room, at this very desk, that—But wait. Let me put it down in black and white, in words simple and unmistakable. Let me ask some questions. Who mislays my pen? That is what I desire to know. Who uses up my ink so rapidly? Not I. And yet the ink goes.

The answer to these questions would settle all the enigmas of the universe. I know the answer. I am not a fool. And some day, if I am plagued too desperately, I shall give the answer myself. I shall give the name of him who mislays my pen and uses up my ink. It is so silly to think that I could use such a quantity of ink. The servant lies. I know.

*   *   *   *   *

I have got me a fountain pen. I have always disliked the device, but my old stub had to go. I burned it in the fireplace. The ink I keep under lock and key. I shall see if I cannot put a stop to these lies that are being written about me. And I have other plans. It is not true that I have recanted. I still believe that I live in a mechanical universe. It has not been proved otherwise to me, for all that I have peered over his shoulder and read his malicious statement to the contrary. He gives me credit for no less than average stupidity. He thinks I think he is real. How silly. I know he is a brain-figment, nothing more.

There are such things as hallucinations. Even as I looked over his shoulder and read, I knew that this was such a thing. If I were only well it would be interesting. All my life I have wanted to experience such phenomena. And now it has come to me. I shall make the most of it. What is imagination? It can make something where there is nothing. How can anything be something where there is nothing? How can anything be something and nothing at the same time? I leave it for the metaphysicians to ponder. I know better. No scholastics for me. This is a real world, and everything in it is real. What is not real, is not. Therefore he is not. Yet he tries to fool me into believing that he is ... when all the time I know he has no existence outside of my own brain cells.

* * * * *

I saw him to-day, seated at the desk, writing. It gave me quite a shock, because I had thought he was quite dispelled. Nevertheless, on looking steadily, I found that he was not there—the old familiar trick of the brain. I have dwelt too long on what has happened. I am becoming morbid, and my old indigestion is hinting and muttering. I shall take exercise. Each day I shall walk for two hours.

* * * * *

It is impossible. I cannot exercise. Each time I return from my walk, he is sitting in my chair at the desk. It grows more difficult to drive him away. It is my chair. Upon this I insist. It *was* his, but he is dead and it is no longer his. How one can be befooled by the phantoms of his own imagining! There is nothing real in this apparition. I know it. I am firmly grounded with my fifty years of study. The dead are dead.

* * * * *

And yet, explain one thing. To-day, before going for my walk, I carefully put the fountain pen in my pocket before leaving the room. I remember it distinctly. I looked at the clock at the time. It was twenty minutes past ten. Yet on my return there was the pen lying on the desk. Some one had been using it. There was very little ink left. I wish he would not write so much. It is disconcerting.

* * * * *

There was one thing upon which Jim and I were not quite agreed. He believed in the eternity of the forms of things. Therefore, entered in immediately the consequent belief in immortality, and all the other notions of the metaphysical philosophers. I had little patience with him in this.

Painstakingly I have traced to him the evolution of his belief in the eternity of forms, showing him how it has arisen out of his early infatuation with logic and mathematics. Of course, from that warped, squinting, abstract view-point, it is very easy to believe in the eternity of forms.

I laughed at the unseen world. Only the real was real, I contended, and what one did not perceive, was not, could not be. I believed in a mechanical universe. Chemistry and physics explained everything. "Can no being be?" he demanded in reply. I said that his question was but the major promise of a fallacious Christian Science syllogism. Oh, believe me, I know my logic, too. But he was very stubborn. I never had any patience with philosophic idealists.

*   *   *   *   *

Once, I made to him my confession of faith. It was simple, brief, unanswerable. Even as I write it now I know that it is unanswerable. Here it is. I told him: "I assert, with Hobbes, that it is impossible to separate thought from matter that thinks. I assert, with Bacon, that all human understanding arises from the world of sensations. I assert, with Locke, that all human ideas are due to the functions of the senses. I assert, with Kant, the mechanical origin of the universe, and that creation is a natural and historical process. I assert, with Laplace, that there is no need of the hypothesis of a creator. And, finally, I assert, because of all the foregoing, that form is ephemeral. Form passes. Therefore we pass."

I repeat, it was unanswerable. Yet did he answer with Paley's notorious fallacy of the watch. Also, he talked about radium, and all but asserted that the very existence of matter had been exploded by these later-day laboratory researches. It was childish. I had not dreamed he could be so immature.

How could one argue with such a man? I then asserted the reasonableness of all that is. To this he agreed, reserving, however, one exception. He looked at me, as he said it, in a way I could not mistake. The inference was obvious. That he should be guilty of so cheap a quip in the midst of a serious discussion, astounded me.

*   *   *   *   *

The eternity of forms. It is ridiculous. Yet is there a strange magic in the words. If it be true, then has he not ceased to exist. Then does he exist. This is impossible.

*   *   *   *   *

I have ceased exercising. As long as I remain in the room, the hallucination does not bother me. But when I return to the room after an absence, he is always there, sitting at the desk, writing. Yet I dare not confide in a physician. I must fight this out by myself.

*   *   *   *   *

He grows more importunate. To-day, consulting a book on the shelf, I turned and found him again in the chair. This is the first time he has dared do this in my presence. Nevertheless, by looking at him steadily and sternly for several minutes, I compelled him to vanish. This proves my contention. He does not exist. If he were an eternal form I could not make him vanish by a mere effort of my will.

*   *   *   *   *

This is getting damnable. To-day I gazed at him for an entire hour before I could make him leave. Yet it is so simple. What I see is a memory picture. For twenty years I was accustomed to seeing him there at the desk. The present phenomenon is merely a recrudescence of that memory picture—a picture which was impressed countless times on my consciousness.

*   *   *   *   *

I gave up to-day. He exhausted me, and still he would not go. I sat and watched him hour after hour. He takes no notice of me, but continually writes. I know what he writes, for I read it over his shoulder. It is not true. He is taking an unfair advantage.

*   *   *   *   *

Query: He is a product of my consciousness; is it possible, then, that entities may be created by consciousness?

*   *   *   *   *

We did not quarrel. To this day I do not know how it happened. Let me tell you. Then you will see. We sat up late that never-to-be-forgotten last night of his existence. It was the old, old discussion—the eternity of forms. How many hours and how many nights we had consumed over it!

On this night he had been particularly irritating, and all my nerves were screaming. He had been maintaining that the human soul was itself a form, an eternal form, and that the light within his brain would go on forever and always. I took up the poker.

"Suppose," I said, "I should strike you dead with this?"

"I would go on," he answered.

"As a conscious entity?" I demanded.

"Yes, as a conscious entity," was his reply. "I should go on, from plane to plane of higher existence, remembering my earth-life, you, this very argument—ay, and continuing the argument with you."

It was only argument[1]. I swear it was only argument. I never lifted a hand. How could I? He was my brother, my elder brother, Jim.

I cannot remember. I was very exasperated. He had always been so obstinate in this metaphysical belief of his. The next I knew, he was lying on the hearth. Blood was running. It was terrible. He did not speak. He did not move. He must have fallen in a fit and struck his head. I noticed there was blood on the poker. In falling he must have struck upon it with his head. And yet I fail to see how this can be, for I held it in my hand all the time. I was still holding it in my hand as I looked at it.

[Footnote 1: (Forcible—ha! ha!—comment of Rudolph Heckler on margin.)]

* * * * *

It is an hallucination. That is a conclusion of common sense. I have watched the growth of it. At first it was only in the dimmest light that I could see him sitting in the chair. But as the time passed, and the hallucination, by repetition, strengthened, he was able to appear in the chair under the strongest lights. That is the explanation. It is quite satisfactory.

* * * * *

I shall never forget the first time I saw it. I had dined alone downstairs. I never drink wine, so that what happened was eminently normal. It was in the summer twilight that I returned to the study. I glanced at the desk. There he was, sitting. So natural was it, that before I knew I cried out "Jim!" Then I remembered all that had happened. Of course it was an hallucination. I knew that. I took the poker and went over to it. He did not move nor vanish. The poker cleaved through the non-existent substance of the thing and struck the back of the chair. Fabric of fancy, that is all it was. The mark is there on the chair now where the poker struck. I pause from my writing and turn and look at it—press the tips of my fingers into the indentation.

* * * * *

He *did* continue the argument. I stole up to-day and looked over his shoulder. He was writing the history of our discussion. It was the same old nonsense about the eternity of forms. But as I continued to read, he wrote down the practical test I had made with the poker. Now this is unfair and untrue. I made no test. In falling he struck his head on the poker.

*　*　*　*　*

Some day, somebody will find and read what he writes. This will be terrible. I am suspicious of the servant, who is always peeping and peering, trying to see what I write. I must do something. Every servant I have had is curious about what I write.

*　*　*　*　*

Fabric of fancy. That is all it is. There is no Jim who sits in the chair. I know that. Last night, when the house was asleep, I went down into the cellar and looked carefully at the soil around the chimney. It was untampered with. The dead do not rise up.

*　*　*　*　*

Yesterday morning, when I entered the study, there he was in the chair. When I had dispelled him, I sat in the chair myself all day. I had my meals brought to me. And thus I escaped the sight of him for many hours, for he appears only in the chair. I was weary, but I sat late, until eleven o'clock. Yet, when I stood up to go to bed, I looked around, and there he was. He had slipped into the chair on the instant. Being only fabric of fancy, all day he had resided in my brain. The moment it was unoccupied, he took up his residence in the chair. Are these his boasted higher planes of existence—his brother's brain and a chair? After all, was he not right? Has his eternal form become so attenuated as to be an hallucination? Are hallucinations real entities? Why not? There is food for thought here. Some day I shall come to a conclusion upon it.

* * * * *

He was very much disturbed to-day. He could not write, for I had made the servant carry the pen out of the room in his pocket But neither could I write.

* * * * *

The servant never sees him. This is strange. Have I developed a keener sight for the unseen? Or rather does it not prove the phantom to be what it is—a product of my own morbid consciousness?

* * * * *

He has stolen my pen again. Hallucinations cannot steal pens. This is unanswerable. And yet I cannot keep the pen always out of the room. I want to write myself.

* * * * *

I have had three different servants since my trouble came upon me, and not one has seen him. Is the verdict of their senses right? And is that of mine wrong? Nevertheless, the ink goes too rapidly. I fill my pen more often than is necessary. And furthermore, only to-day I found my pen out of order. I did not break it.

* * * * *

I have spoken to him many times, but he never answers. I sat and watched him all morning. Frequently he looked at me, and it was patent that he knew me.

* * * * *

By striking the side of my head violently with the heel of my hand, I can shake the vision of him out of my eyes. Then I can get into the chair; but I have learned that I must move very quickly in order to accomplish this. Often he fools me and is back again before I can sit down.

*　　*　　*　　*　　*

It is getting unbearable. He is a jack-in-the-box the way he pops into the chair. He does not assume form slowly. He pops. That is the only way to describe it. I cannot stand looking at him much more. That way lies madness, for it compels me almost to believe in the reality of what I know is not. Besides, hallucinations do not pop.

*　　*　　*　　*　　*

Thank God he only manifests himself in the chair. As long as I occupy the chair I am quit of him.

*　　*　　*　　*　　*

My device for dislodging him from the chair by striking my head, is failing. I have to hit much more violently, and I do not succeed perhaps more than once in a dozen trials. My head is quite sore where I have so repeatedly struck it. I must use the other hand.

*　　*　　*　　*　　*

My brother was right. There is an unseen world. Do I not see it? Am I not cursed with the seeing of it all the time? Call it a thought, an idea, anything you will, still it is there. It is unescapable. Thoughts are entities. We create with every act of thinking. I have created this phantom that sits in my chair and uses my ink. Because I have created him is no reason that he is any the less real. He is an idea; he is an entity: ergo, ideas are entities, and an entity is a reality.

*　　*　　*　　*　　*

Query: If a man, with the whole historical process behind him, can create an entity, a real thing, then is not the hypothesis of a Creator made substantial? If the stuff of life can create, then it is fair to assume that there can be a He who created the stuff of life. It is merely a difference of degree. I have not yet made a mountain nor a solar system, but I have made a something that sits in my chair. This being so, may I not some day be able to make a mountain or a solar system?

* * * * *

All his days, down to to-day, man has lived in a maze. He has never seen the light. I am convinced that I am beginning to see the light—not as my brother saw it, by stumbling upon it accidentally, but deliberately and rationally. My brother is dead. He has ceased. There is no doubt about it, for I have made another journey down into the cellar to see. The ground was untouched. I broke it myself to make sure, and I saw what made me sure. My brother has ceased, yet have I recreated him. This is not my old brother, yet it is something as nearly resembling him as I could fashion it. I am unlike other men. I am a god. I have created.

* * * * *

Whenever I leave the room to go to bed, I look back, and there is my brother sitting in the chair. And then I cannot sleep because of thinking of him sitting through all the long night-hours. And in the morning, when I open the study door, there he is, and I know he has sat there the night long.

* * * * *

I am becoming desperate from lack of sleep. I wish I could confide in a physician.

* * * * *

Blessed sleep! I have won to it at last. Let me tell you. Last night I was so worn that I found myself dozing in my chair. I rang for the servant and ordered him to bring blankets. I slept. All night was he banished from my thoughts as he was banished from my chair. I shall remain in it all day. It is a wonderful relief.

*   *   *   *   *

It is uncomfortable to sleep in a chair. But it is more uncomfortable to lie in bed, hour after hour, and not sleep, and to know that he is sitting there in the cold darkness.

*   *   *   *   *

It is no use. I shall never be able to sleep in a bed again. I have tried it now, numerous times, and every such night is a horror. If I could but only persuade him to go to bed! But no. He sits there, and sits there—I know he does—while I stare and stare up into the blackness and think and think, continually think, of him sitting there. I wish I had never heard of the eternity of forms.

*   *   *   *   *

The servants think I am crazy. That is but to be expected, and it is why I have never called in a physician.

*   *   *   *   *

I am resolved. Henceforth this hallucination ceases. From now on I shall remain in the chair. I shall never leave it. I shall remain in it night and day and always.

*   *   *   *   *

I have succeeded. For two weeks I have not seen him. Nor shall I ever see him again. I have at last attained the equanimity of mind necessary for philosophic thought. I wrote a complete chapter to-day.

*   *   *   *   *

It is very wearisome, sitting in a chair. The weeks pass, the months come and go, the seasons change, the servants replace each other, while I remain. I only remain. It is a strange life I lead, but at least I am at peace.

*   *   *   *   *

He comes no more. There is no eternity of forms. I have proved it. For nearly two years now, I have remained in this chair, and I have not seen him once. True, I was severely tried for a time. But it is clear that what I thought I saw was merely hallucination. He never was. Yet I do not leave the chair. I am afraid to leave the chair.

TOLD IN THE DROOLING WARD

Me? I'm not a drooler. I'm the assistant, I don't know what Miss Jones or Miss Kelsey could do without me. There are fifty-five low-grade droolers in this ward, and how could they ever all be fed if I wasn't around? I like to feed droolers. They don't make trouble. They can't. Something's wrong with most of their legs and arms, and they can't talk. They're very low-grade. I can walk, and talk, and do things. You must be careful with the droolers and not feed them too fast. Then they choke. Miss Jones says I'm an expert. When a new nurse comes I show her how to do it. It's funny watching a new nurse try to feed them. She goes at it so slow and careful that supper time would be around before she finished shoving down their breakfast. Then I show her, because I'm an expert. Dr. Dalrymple says I am, and he ought to know. A drooler can eat twice as fast if you know how to make him.

My name's Tom. I'm twenty-eight years old. Everybody knows me in the institution. This is an institution, you know. It belongs to the State of California and is run by politics. I know. I've been here a long time. Everybody trusts me. I run errands all over the place, when I'm not busy with the droolers. I like droolers. It makes me think how lucky I am that I ain't a drooler.

I like it here in the Home. I don't like the outside. I know. I've been around a bit, and run away, and adopted. Me for the Home, and for the drooling ward best of all. I don't look like a drooler, do I? You can tell the difference soon as you look at me. I'm an assistant, expert assistant. That's going some for a feeb. Feeb? Oh, that's feeble-minded. I thought you knew. We're all feebs in here.

But I'm a high-grade feeb. Dr. Dalrymple says I'm too smart to be in the Home, but I never let on. It's a pretty good place. And I don't throw fits like lots of the feebs. You see that house up there through the trees. The high-grade epilecs all live in it by themselves. They're stuck up because they ain't just ordinary feebs. They call it the club house, and they say they're just as good as anybody outside, only they're sick. I don't like them much. They laugh at me, when they ain't busy throwing fits. But I don't care. I never have to be scared about falling down and busting my head. Sometimes they run around in circles trying to find a place to sit down quick, only they don't. Low-grade epilecs are disgusting, and high-grade epilecs put on airs. I'm glad I ain't an epilec. There ain't anything to them. They just talk big, that's all.

Miss Kelsey says I talk too much. But I talk sense, and that's more than the other feebs do. Dr. Dalrymple says I have the gift of language. I know it. You ought to hear me talk when I'm by myself, or when I've got a drooler to listen. Sometimes I think I'd like to be a politician, only it's too much trouble. They're all great talkers; that's how they hold their jobs.

Nobody's crazy in this institution. They're just feeble in their minds. Let me tell you something funny. There's about a dozen high-grade girls that set the tables in the big dining room. Sometimes when they're done ahead of time, they all sit down in chairs in a circle and talk. I sneak up to the door and listen, and I nearly die to keep from laughing. Do you want to know what they talk? It's like this. They don't say a word for a long time. And then one says, "Thank God I'm not feeble-minded." And all the rest nod their heads and look pleased. And then nobody says anything for a time. After which the next girl in the circle says, "Thank God I'm not feeble-minded," and they nod their heads all over again. And it goes on around the circle, and they never say anything else. Now they're real feebs, ain't they? I leave it to you. I'm not that kind of a feeb, thank God.

Sometimes I don't think I'm a feeb at all. I play in the band and read music. We're all supposed to be feebs in the band except the leader. He's crazy. We know it, but we never talk about it except amongst ourselves. His job is politics, too, and we don't want him to lose it. I play the drum. They can't get along without me in this institution. I was sick once, so I know. It's a wonder the drooling ward didn't break down while I was in hospital.

I could get out of here if I wanted to. I'm not so feeble as some might think. But I don't let on. I have too good a time. Besides, everything would run down if I went away. I'm afraid some time they'll find out I'm not a feeb and send me out into the world to earn my own living. I know the world, and I don't like it. The Home is fine enough for me.

You see how I grin sometimes. I can't help that. But I can put it on a lot. I'm not bad, though. I look at myself in the glass. My mouth is funny, I know that, and it lops down, and my teeth are bad. You can tell a feeb anywhere by looking at his mouth and teeth. But that doesn't prove I'm a feeb. It's just because I'm lucky that I look like one.

I know a lot. If I told you all I know, you'd be surprised. But when I don't want to know, or when they want me to do something I don't want to do, I just let my mouth lop down and laugh and make foolish noises. I watch the foolish noises made by the low-grades, and I can fool anybody. And I know a lot of foolish noises. Miss Kelsey called me a fool the other day. She was very angry, and that was where I fooled her.

Miss Kelsey asked me once why I don't write a book about feebs. I was telling her what was the matter with little Albert. He's a drooler, you know, and I can always tell the way he twists his left eye what's the matter with him. So I was explaining it to Miss Kelsey, and, because she didn't know, it made her mad. But some day, mebbe, I'll write that book. Only it's so much trouble. Besides, I'd sooner talk.

Do you know what a micro is? It's the kind with the little heads no bigger than your fist. They're usually droolers, and they live a long time. The hydros don't drool. They have the big heads, and they're smarter. But they never grow up. They always die. I never look at one without thinking he's going to die. Sometimes, when I'm feeling lazy, or the nurse is mad at me, I wish I was a drooler with nothing to do and somebody to feed me. But I guess I'd sooner talk and be what I am.

Only yesterday Doctor Dalrymple said to me, "Tom," he said, "I just don't know what I'd do without you." And he ought to know, seeing as he's had the bossing of a thousand feebs for going on two years. Dr. Whatcomb was before him. They get appointed, you know. It's politics. I've seen a whole lot of doctors here in my time. I was here before any of them. I've been in this institution twenty-five years. No, I've got no complaints. The institution couldn't be run better.

It's a snap to be a high-grade feeb. Just look at Doctor Dalrymple. He has troubles. He holds his job by politics. You bet we high-graders talk politics. We know all about it, and it's bad. An institution like this oughtn't to be run on politics. Look at Doctor Dalrymple. He's been here two years and learned a lot. Then politics will come along and throw him out and send a new doctor who don't know anything about feebs.

I've been acquainted with just thousands of nurses in my time. Some of them are nice. But they come and go. Most of the women get married. Sometimes I think I'd like to get married. I spoke to Dr. Whatcomb about it once, but he told me he was very sorry, because feebs ain't allowed to get married. I've been in love. She was a nurse. I won't tell you her name. She had blue eyes, and yellow hair, and a kind voice, and she liked me. She told me so. And she always told me to be a good boy. And I was, too, until afterward, and then I ran away. You see, she went off and got married, and she didn't tell me about it.

I guess being married ain't what it's cracked up to be. Dr. Anglin and his wife used to fight. I've seen them. And once I heard her call him a feeb. Now nobody has a right to call anybody a feeb that ain't. Dr. Anglin got awful mad when she called him that. But he didn't last long. Politics drove him out, and Doctor Mandeville came. He didn't have a wife. I heard him talking one time with the engineer. The engineer and his wife fought like cats and dogs, and that day Doctor Mandeville told him he was damn glad he wasn't tied to no petticoats. A petticoat is a skirt. I knew what he meant, if I was a feeb. But I never let on. You hear lots when you don't let on.

I've seen a lot in my time. Once I was adopted, and went away on the railroad over forty miles to live with a man named Peter Bopp and his wife. They had a ranch. Doctor Anglin said I was strong and bright, and I said I was, too. That was because I wanted to be adopted. And Peter Bopp said he'd give me a good home, and the lawyers fixed up the papers.

But I soon made up my mind that a ranch was no place for me. Mrs. Bopp was scared to death of me and wouldn't let me sleep in the house. They fixed up the woodshed and made me sleep there. I had to get up at four o'clock and feed the horses, and milk cows, and carry the milk to the neighbours. They called it chores, but it kept me going all day. I chopped wood, and cleaned chicken houses, and weeded vegetables, and did most everything on the place. I never had any fun. I hadn't no time.

Let me tell you one thing. I'd sooner feed mush and milk to feebs than milk cows with the frost on the ground. Mrs. Bopp was scared to let me play with her children. And I was scared, too. They used to make faces at me when nobody was looking, and call me "Looney." Everybody called me Looney Tom. And the other boys in the neighbourhood threw rocks at me. You never see anything like that in the Home here. The feebs are better behaved.

Mrs. Bopp used to pinch me and pull my hair when she

thought I was too slow, and I only made foolish noises and went slower. She said I'd be the death of her some day. I left the boards off the old well in the pasture, and the pretty new calf fell in and got drowned. Then Peter Bopp said he was going to give me a licking. He did, too. He took a strap halter and went at me. It was awful. I'd never had a licking in my life. They don't do such things in the Home, which is why I say the Home is the place for me.

I know the law, and I knew he had no right to lick me with a strap halter. That was being cruel, and the guardianship papers said he mustn't be cruel. I didn't say anything. I just waited, which shows you what kind of a feeb I am. I waited a long time, and got slower, and made more foolish noises; but he wouldn't, send me back to the Home, which was what I wanted. But one day, it was the first of the month, Mrs. Brown gave me three dollars, which was for her milk bill with Peter Bopp. That was in the morning. When I brought the milk in the evening I was to bring back the receipt. But I didn't. I just walked down to the station, bought a ticket like any one, and rode on the train back to the Home. That's the kind of a feeb I am.

Doctor Anglin was gone then, and Doctor Mandeville had his place. I walked right into his office. He didn't know me. "Hello," he said, "this ain't visiting day." "I ain't a visitor," I said. "I'm Tom. I belong here." Then he whistled and showed he was surprised. I told him all about it, and showed him the marks of the strap halter, and he got madder and madder all the time and said he'd attend to Mr. Peter Bopp's case.

And mebbe you think some of them little droolers weren't glad to see me.

I walked right into the ward. There was a new nurse feeding little Albert. "Hold on," I said. "That ain't the way. Don't you see how he's twisting that left eye? Let me show you." Mebbe she thought I was a new doctor, for she just gave me the spoon, and I guess I filled little Albert up with the most comfortable meal he'd had since I went away. Droolers ain't bad when you understand them. I heard Miss Jones tell Miss Kelsey once that I had an amazing gift in handling droolers.

Some day, mebbe, I'm going to talk with Doctor Dalrymple and get him to give me a declaration that I ain't a feeb. Then I'll get him to make me a real assistant in the drooling ward, with forty dollars a month and my board. And then I'll marry Miss Jones and live right on here. And if she won't have me, I'll marry Miss Kelsey or some other nurse. There's lots of them that want to get married. And I won't care if my wife gets mad and calls me a feeb. What's the good? And I guess when one's learned to put up with droolers a wife won't be much worse.

I didn't tell you about when I ran away. I hadn't no idea of such a thing and it was Charley and Joe who put me up to it. They're high-grade epilecs, you know. I'd been up to Doctor Wilson's office with a message, and was going back to the drooling ward, when I saw Charley and Joe hiding around the corner of the gymnasium and making motions to me. I went over to them.

"Hello," Joe said. "How's droolers?"

"Fine," I said. "Had any fits lately?"

That made them mad, and I was going on, when Joe said, "We're running away. Come on."

"What for?" I said.

"We're going up over the top of the mountain," Joe said.

"And find a gold mine," said Charley. "We don't have fits any more. We're cured."

"All right," I said. And we sneaked around back of the gymnasium and in among the trees. Mebbe we walked along about ten minutes, when I stopped.

"What's the matter?" said Joe.

"Wait," I said. "I got to go back."

"What for?" said Joe.

And I said, "To get little Albert."

And they said I couldn't, and got mad. But I didn't care. I knew they'd wait. You see, I've been here twenty-five years, and I know the back trails that lead up the mountain, and Charley and Joe didn't know those trails. That's why they wanted me to come.

So I went back and got little Albert. He can't walk, or talk, or do anything except drool, and I had to carry him in my arms. We went on past the last hayfield, which was as far as I'd ever gone. Then the woods and brush got so thick, and me not finding any more trail, we followed the cow-path down to a big creek and crawled through the fence which showed where the Home land stopped.

We climbed up the big hill on the other side of the creek. It was all big trees, and no brush, but it was so steep and slippery with dead leaves we could hardly walk. By and by we came to a real bad place. It was forty feet across, and if you slipped you'd fall a thousand feet, or mebbe a hundred. Anyway, you wouldn't fall—just slide. I went across first, carrying little Albert. Joe came next. But Charley got scared right in the middle and sat down.

"I'm going to have a fit," he said.

"No, you're not," said Joe. "Because if you was you wouldn't 'a' sat down. You take all your fits standing."

"This is a different kind of a fit," said Charley, beginning to cry.

He shook and shook, but just because he wanted to he couldn't scare up the least kind of a fit.

Joe got mad and used awful language. But that didn't help none. So I talked soft and kind to Charley. That's the way to handle feebs. If you get mad, they get worse. I know. I'm that way myself. That's why I was almost the death of Mrs. Bopp. She got mad.

It was getting along in the afternoon, and I knew we had to be on our way, so I said to Joe:

"Here, stop your cussing and hold Albert. I'll go back and get him."

And I did, too; but he was so scared and dizzy he crawled along on hands and knees while I helped him. When I got him across and took Albert back in my arms, I heard somebody laugh and looked down. And there was a man and woman on horseback looking up at us. He had a gun on his saddle, and it was her who was laughing.

"Who in hell's that?" said Joe, getting scared. "Somebody to catch us?"

"Shut up your cussing," I said to him. "That is the man who owns this ranch and writes books."

"How do you do, Mr. Endicott," I said down to him.

"Hello," he said. "What are you doing here?"

"We're running away," I said.

And he said, "Good luck. But be sure and get back before dark."

"But this is a real running away," I said.

And then both he and his wife laughed.

"All right," he said. "Good luck just the same. But watch out the bears and mountain lions don't get you when it gets dark."

Then they rode away laughing, pleasant like; but I wished he hadn't said that about the bears and mountain lions.

After we got around the hill, I found a trail, and we went much faster. Charley didn't have any more signs of fits, and began laughing and talking about gold mines. The trouble was with little Albert. He was almost as big as me. You see, all the time I'd been calling him little Albert, he'd been growing up. He was so heavy I couldn't keep up with Joe and Charley. I was all out of breath. So I told them they'd have to take turns in carrying him, which they said they wouldn't. Then I said I'd leave them and they'd get lost, and the mountain lions and bears would eat them. Charley looked like he was going to have a fit right there, and Joe said, "Give him to me." And after that we carried him in turn.

We kept right on up that mountain. I don't think there was any gold mine, but we might 'a' got to the top and found it, if we hadn't lost the trail, and if it hadn't got dark, and if little Albert hadn't tired us all out carrying him. Lots of feebs are scared of the dark, and Joe said he was going to have a fit right there. Only he didn't. I never saw such an unlucky boy. He never could throw a fit when he wanted to. Some of the feebs can throw fits as quick as a wink.

By and by it got real black, and we were hungry, and we didn't have no fire. You see, they don't let feebs carry matches, and all we could do was just shiver. And we'd never thought about being hungry. You see, feebs always have their food ready for them, and that's why it's better to be a feeb than earning your living in the world.

And worse than everything was the quiet. There was only one thing worse, and it was the noises. There was all kinds of noises every once in a while, with quiet spells in between. I reckon they were rabbits, but they made noises in the brush like wild animals—you know, rustle rustle, thump, bump, crackle crackle, just like that. First Charley got a fit, a real one, and Joe threw a terrible one. I don't mind fits in the Home with everybody around. But out in the woods on a dark night is different. You listen to me, and never go hunting gold mines with epilecs, even if they are high-grade.

I never had such an awful night. When Joe and Charley weren't throwing fits they were making believe, and in the darkness the shivers from the cold which I couldn't see seemed like fits, too. And I shivered so hard I thought I was getting fits myself. And little Albert, with nothing to eat, just drooled and drooled. I never seen him as bad as that before. Why, he twisted that left eye of his until it ought to have dropped out. I couldn't see it, but I could tell from the movements he made. And Joe just lay and cussed and cussed, and Charley cried and wished he was back in the Home.

We didn't die, and next morning we went right back the way we'd come. And little Albert got awful heavy. Doctor Wilson was mad as could be, and said I was the worst feeb in the institution, along with Joe and Charley. But Miss Striker, who was a nurse in the drooling ward then, just put her arms around me and cried, she was that happy I'd got back. I thought right there that mebbe I'd marry her. But only a month afterward she got married to the plumber that came up from the city to fix the gutter-pipes of the new hospital. And little Albert never twisted his eye for two days, it was that tired.

Next time I run away I'm going right over that mountain. But I ain't going to take epilecs along. They ain't never cured, and when they get scared or excited they throw fits to beat the band. But I'll take little Albert. Somehow I can't get along without him. And anyway, I ain't going to run away. The drooling ward's a better snap than gold mines, and I hear there's a new nurse coming. Besides, little Albert's bigger than I am now, and I could never carry him over a mountain. And he's growing bigger every day. It's astonishing.

THE HOBO AND THE FAIRY

He lay on his back. So heavy was his sleep that the stamp of hoofs and cries of the drivers from the bridge that crossed the creek did not rouse him. Wagon after wagon, loaded high with grapes, passed the bridge on the way up the valley to the winery, and the coming of each wagon was like an explosion of sound and commotion in the lazy quiet of the afternoon.

But the man was undisturbed. His head had slipped from the folded newspaper, and the straggling unkempt hair was matted with the foxtails and burrs of the dry grass on which it lay. He was not a pretty sight. His mouth was open, disclosing a gap in the upper row where several teeth at some time had been knocked out. He breathed stertorously, at times grunting and moaning with the pain of his sleep. Also, he was very restless, tossing his arms about, making jerky, half-convulsive movements, and at times rolling his head from side to side in the burrs. This restlessness seemed occasioned partly by some internal discomfort, and partly by the sun that streamed down on his face and by the flies that buzzed and lighted and crawled upon the nose and cheeks and eyelids. There was no other place for them to crawl, for the rest of the face was covered with matted beard, slightly grizzled, but greatly dirt-stained and weather-discoloured.

The cheek-bones were blotched with the blood congested by the debauch that was evidently being slept off. This, too, accounted for the persistence with which the flies clustered around the mouth, lured by the alcohol-laden exhalations. He was a powerfully built man, thick-necked, broad-shouldered, with sinewy wrists and toil-distorted hands. Yet the distortion was not due to recent toil, nor were the callouses other than ancient that showed under the dirt of the one palm upturned. From time to time this hand clenched tightly and spasmodically into a fist, large, heavy-boned and wicked-looking.

The man lay in the dry grass of a tiny glade that ran down to the tree-fringed bank of the stream. On either side of the glade was a fence, of the old stake-and-rider type, though little of it was to be seen, so thickly was it overgrown by wild blackberry bushes, scrubby oaks and young madrono trees. In the rear, a gate through a low paling fence led to a snug, squat bungalow, built in the California Spanish style and seeming to have been compounded directly from the landscape of which it was so justly a part. Neat and trim and modestly sweet was the bungalow, redolent of comfort and repose, telling with quiet certitude of some one that knew, and that had sought and found.

Through the gate and into the glade came as dainty a little maiden as ever stepped out of an illustration made especially to show how dainty little maidens may be. Eight years she might have been, and, possibly, a trifle more, or less. Her little waist and little black-stockinged calves showed how delicately fragile she was; but the fragility was of mould only. There was no hint of anaemia in the clear, healthy complexion nor in the quick, tripping step. She was a little, delicious blond, with hair spun of gossamer gold and wide blue eyes that were but slightly veiled by the long lashes. Her expression was of sweetness and happiness; it belonged by right to any face that sheltered in the bungalow.

She carried a child's parasol, which she was careful not to tear against the scrubby branches and bramble bushes as she sought for wild poppies along the edge of the fence. They were late poppies, a third generation, which had been unable to resist the call of the warm October sun.

Having gathered along one fence, she turned to cross to the opposite fence. Midway in the glade she came upon the tramp. Her startle was merely a startle. There was no fear in it. She stood and looked long and curiously at the forbidding spectacle, and was about to turn back when the sleeper moved restlessly and rolled his hand among the burrs. She noted the sun on his face, and the buzzing flies; her face grew solicitous, and for a moment she debated with herself. Then she tiptoed to his side, interposed the parasol between him and the sun, and brushed away the flies. After a time, for greater ease, she sat down beside him.

An hour passed, during which she occasionally shifted the parasol from one tired hand to the other. At first the sleeper had been restless, but, shielded from the flies and the sun, his breathing became gentler and his movements ceased. Several times, however, he really frightened her. The first was the worst, coming abruptly and without warning. "Christ! How deep! How deep!" the man murmured from some profound of dream. The parasol was agitated; but the little girl controlled herself and continued her self-appointed ministrations.

Another time it was a gritting of teeth, as of some intolerable agony. So terribly did the teeth crunch and grind together that it seemed they must crash into fragments. A little later he suddenly stiffened out. The hands clenched and the face set with the savage resolution of the dream. The eyelids trembled from the shock of the fantasy, seemed about to open, but did not. Instead, the lips muttered:

"No; by God, no. And once more no. I won't peach." The lips paused, then went on. "You might as well tie me up, warden, and cut me to pieces. That's all you can get outa me—blood. That's all any of you-uns has ever got outa me in this hole."

After this outburst the man slept gently on, while the little girl still held the parasol aloft and looked down with a great wonder at the frowsy, unkempt creature, trying to reconcile it with the little part of life that she knew. To her ears came the cries of men, the stamp of hoofs on the bridge, and the creak and groan of wagons heavy-laden. It was a breathless California Indian summer day. Light fleeces of cloud drifted in the azure sky, but to the west heavy cloud banks threatened with rain. A bee droned lazily by. From farther thickets came the calls of quail, and from the fields the songs of meadow larks. And oblivious to it all slept Ross Shanklin—Ross Shanklin, the tramp and outcast, ex-convict 4379, the bitter and unbreakable one who had defied all keepers and survived all brutalities.

Texas-born, of the old pioneer stock that was always tough and stubborn, he had been unfortunate. At seventeen years of age he had been apprehended for horse-stealing. Also, he had been convicted of stealing seven horses which he had not stolen, and he had been sentenced to fourteen years' imprisonment. This was severe under any circumstances, but with him it had been especially severe, because there had been no prior convictions against him. The sentiment of the people who believed him guilty had been that two years was adequate punishment for the youth, but the county attorney, paid according to the convictions he secured, had made seven charges against him and earned seven fees. Which goes to show that the county attorney valued twelve years of Ross Shanklin's life at less than a few dollars.

Young Ross Shanklin had toiled in hell; he had escaped, more than once; and he had been caught and sent back to toil in other and various hells. He had been triced up and lashed till he fainted, had been revived and lashed again. He had been in the dungeon ninety days at a time. He had experienced the torment of the straightjacket. He knew what the humming bird was. He had been farmed out as a chattel by the state to the contractors. He had been trailed through swamps by blood hounds. Twice he had been shot. For six years on end he had cut a cord and a half of wood each day in a convict lumber camp. Sick or well, he had cut that cord and a half or paid for it under a whip-lash knotted and pickled.

And Ross Shanklin had not sweetened under the treatment. He had sneered, and cursed, and defied. He had seen convicts, after the guards had manhandled them, crippled in body for life, or left to maunder in mind to the end of their days. He had seen convicts, even his own cell-mate, goaded to murder by their keepers, go to the gallows cursing God. He had been in a break in which eleven of his kind were shot down. He had been through a mutiny, where, in the prison yard, with gatling guns trained upon them, three hundred convicts had been disciplined with pick-handles wielded by brawny guards.

He had known every infamy of human cruelty, and through it all he had never been broken. He had resented and fought to the last, until, embittered and bestial, the day came when he was discharged. Five dollars were given him in payment for the years of his labour and the flower of his manhood. And he had worked little in the years that followed. Work he hated and despised. He tramped, begged and stole, lied or threatened as the case might warrant, and drank to besottedness whenever he got the chance.

The little girl was looking at him when he awoke. Like a wild animal, all of him was awake the instant he opened his eyes. The first he saw was the parasol, strangely obtruded between him and the sky. He did not start nor move, though his whole body seemed slightly to tense. His eyes followed down the parasol handle to the tight-clutched little fingers, and along the arm to the child's face. Straight and unblinking, he looked into her eyes, and she, returning the look, was chilled and frightened by his glittering eyes, cold and harsh, withal bloodshot, and with no hint in them of the warm humanness she had been accustomed to see and feel in human eyes. They were the true prison eyes—the eyes of a man who had learned to talk little, who had forgotten almost how to talk.

"Hello," he said finally, making no effort to change his position. "What game are you up to?"

His voice was gruff and husky, and at first it had been harsh;

but it had softened queerly in a feeble attempt at forgotten kindliness.

"How do you do?" she said. "I'm not playing. The sun was on your face, and mamma says one oughtn't to sleep in the sun."

The sweet clearness of her child's voice was pleasant to him, and he wondered why he had never noticed it in children's voices before. He sat up slowly and stared at her. He felt that he ought to say something, but speech with him was a reluctant thing.

"I hope you slept well," she said gravely.

"I sure did," he answered, never taking his eyes from her, amazed at the fairness and delicacy of her. "How long was you holdin' that contraption up over me?"

"O-oh," she debated with herself, "a long, long time. I thought you would never wake up."

"And I thought you was a fairy when I first seen you."

He felt elated at his contribution to the conversation.

"No, not a fairy," she smiled.

He thrilled in a strange, numb way at the immaculate whiteness of her small even teeth.

"I was just the good Samaritan," she added.

"I reckon I never heard of that party."

He was cudgelling his brains to keep the conversation going. Never having been at close quarters with a child since he was man-grown, he found it difficult.

"What a funny man not to know about the good Samaritan.

Don't you remember? A certain man went down to Jericho—"

"I reckon I've been there," he interrupted.

"I knew you were a traveller!" she cried, clapping her hands. "Maybe you saw the exact spot."

"What spot?'

"Why, where he fell among thieves and was left half dead. And then the good Samaritan went to him, and bound up his wounds, and poured in oil and wine—was that olive oil, do you think?"

He shook his head slowly.

"I reckon you got me there. Olive oil is something the dagoes cooks with. I never heard of it for busted heads."

She considered his statement for a moment.

"Well," she announced, "we use olive oil in our cooking, so we must be dagoes. I never knew what they were before. I thought it was slang."

"And the Samaritan dumped oil on his head," the tramp muttered reminiscently. "Seems to me I recollect a sky pilot sayin' something about that old gent. D'ye know, I've been looking for him off'n' on all my life, and never scared up hide or hair of him. They ain't no more Samaritans."

"Wasn't I one?" she asked quickly.

He looked at her steadily, with a great curiosity and wonder. Her ear, by a movement exposed to the sun, was transparent. It seemed he could almost see through it. He was amazed at the delicacy of her colouring, at the blue of her eyes, at the dazzle of the sun-touched golden hair. And he was astounded by her fragility. It came to him that she was easily broken. His eye went quickly from his huge, gnarled paw to her tiny hand in which it seemed to him he could almost see the blood circulate. He knew the power in his muscles, and he knew the tricks and turns by which men use their bodies to ill-treat men. In fact, he knew little else, and his mind for the time ran in its customary channel. It was his way of measuring the beautiful strangeness of her. He calculated a grip, and not a strong one, that could grind her little fingers to pulp. He thought of fist-blows he had given to men's heads, and received on his own head, and felt that the least of them could shatter hers like an eggshell. He scanned her little shoulders and slim waist, and knew in all certitude that with his two hands he could rend her to pieces.

"Wasn't I one?" she insisted again.

He came back to himself with a shock—or away from himself, as the case happened. He was loth that the conversation should cease.

"What?" he answered. "Oh, yes; you bet you was a Samaritan, even if you didn't have no olive oil." He remembered what his mind had been dwelling on, and asked, "But ain't you afraid?"

She looked at him uncomprehendingly.

"Of ... of me?" he added lamely.

She laughed merrily.

"Mamma says never to be afraid of anything. She says that if you're good, and you think good of other people, they'll be good, too."

"And you was thinkin' good of me when you kept the sun off," he marvelled.

"But it's hard to think good of bees and nasty crawly things," she confessed.

"But there's men that is nasty and crawly things," he argued.

"Mamma says no. She says there's good in every one."

"I bet you she locks the house up tight at night just the same," he proclaimed triumphantly.

"But she doesn't. Mamma isn't afraid of anything. That's why she lets me play out here alone when I want. Why, we had a robber once. Mamma got right up and found him. And what do you think! He was only a poor hungry man. And she got him plenty to eat from the pantry, and afterward she got him work to do."

Ross Shanklin was stunned. The vista shown him of human nature was unthinkable. It had been his lot to live in a world of suspicion and hatred, of evil-believing and evil-doing. It had been his experience, slouching along village streets at nightfall, to see little children, screaming with fear, run from him to their mothers. He had even seen grown women shrink aside from him as he passed along the sidewalk.

He was aroused by the girl clapping her hands as she cried out.

"I know what you are! You're an open air crank. That's why you were sleeping here in the grass."

He felt a grim desire to laugh, but repressed it.

"And that's what tramps are—open air cranks," she continued. "I often wondered. Mamma believes in the open air. I sleep on the porch at night. So does she. This is our land. You must have climbed the fence. Mamma lets me when I put on my climbers—they're bloomers, you know. But you ought to be told something. A person doesn't know when they snore because they're asleep. But you do worse than that. You grit your teeth. That's bad. Whenever you are going to sleep you must think to yourself, 'I won't grit my teeth, I won't grit my teeth,' over and over, just like that, and by and by you'll get out of the habit.

"All bad things are habits. And so are all good things. And it depends on us what kind our habits are going to be. I used to pucker my eyebrows—wrinkle them all up, but mamma said I must overcome that habit. She said that when my eyebrows were wrinkled it was an advertisement that my brain was wrinkled inside, and that it wasn't good to have wrinkles in the brain. And then she smoothed my eyebrows with her hand and said I must always think *smooth—smooth* inside, and *smooth* outside. And do you know, it was easy. I haven't wrinkled my brows for ever so long. I've heard about filling teeth by thinking. But I don't believe that. Neither does mamma."

She paused, rather out of breath. Nor did he speak. Her flow of talk had been too much for him. Also, sleeping drunkenly, with open mouth, had made him very thirsty. But, rather than lose one precious moment, he endured the torment of his scorching throat and mouth. He licked his dry lips and struggled for speech.

"What is your name?" he managed at last.

"Joan."

She looked her own question at him, and it was not necessary to voice it.

"Mine is Ross Shanklin," he volunteered, for the first time in forgotten years giving his real name.

"I suppose you've travelled a lot."

"I sure have, but not as much as I might have wanted to."

"Papa always wanted to travel, but he was too busy at the office. He never could get much time. He went to Europe once with mamma. That was before I was born. It takes money to travel."

Ross Shanklin did not know whether to agree with this statement or not.

"But it doesn't cost tramps much for expenses," she took the thought away from him. "Is that why you tramp?"

He nodded and licked his lips.

"Mamma says it's too bad that men must tramp to look for work. But there's lots of work now in the country. All the farmers in the valley are trying to get men. Have you been working?"

He shook his head, angry with himself that he should feel shame at the confession when his savage reasoning told him he was right in despising work. But this was followed by another thought. This beautiful little creature was some man's child. She was one of the rewards of work.

"I wish I had a little girl like you," he blurted out, stirred by a sudden consciousness of passion for paternity. "I'd work my hands off. I .. I'd do anything."

She considered his case with fitting gravity.

"Then you aren't married?"

"Nobody would have me."

"Yes they would, if...."

She did not turn up her nose, but she favoured his dirt and rags with a look of disapprobation he could not mistake.

"Go on," he half-shouted. "Shoot it into me. If I was washed—if I wore good clothes—if I was respectable—if I had a job and worked regular—if I wasn't what I am."

To each statement she nodded.

"Well, I ain't that kind," he rushed on.

"I'm no good. I'm a tramp. I don't want to work, that's what. And I like dirt."

Her face was eloquent with reproach as she said, "Then you were only making believe when you wished you had a little girl like me?"

This left him speechless, for he knew, in all the deeps of his new-found passion, that that was just what he did want.

With ready tact, noting his discomfort, she sought to change the subject.

"What do you think of God?" she asked.

"I ain't never met him. What do you think about him?"

His reply was evidently angry, and she was frank in her disapproval.

"You are very strange," she said. "You get angry so easily. I never saw anybody before that got angry about God, or work, or being clean."

"He never done anything for me," he muttered resentfully. He cast back in quick review of the long years of toil in the convict camps and mines. "And work never done anything for me neither."

An embarrassing silence fell.

He looked at her, numb and hungry with the stir of the father-love, sorry for his ill temper, puzzling his brain for something to say. She was looking off and away at the clouds, and he devoured her with his eyes. He reached out stealthily and rested one grimy hand on the very edge of her little dress. It seemed to him that she was the most wonderful thing in the world. The quail still called from the coverts, and the harvest sounds seemed abruptly to become very loud. A great loneliness oppressed him.

"I'm ... I'm no good," he murmured huskily and repentantly.

But, beyond a glance from her blue eyes, she took no notice. The silence was more embarrassing than ever. He felt that he could give the world just to touch with his lips that hem of her dress where his hand rested. But he was afraid of frightening her. He fought to find something to say, licking his parched lips and vainly attempting to articulate something, anything.

"This ain't Sonoma Valley," he declared finally. "This is fairy land, and you're a fairy. Mebbe I'm asleep and dreaming. I don't know. You and me don't know how to talk together, because, you see, you're a fairy and don't know nothing but good things, and I'm a man from the bad, wicked world."

Having achieved this much, he was left gasping for ideas like a stranded fish.

"And you're going to tell me about the bad, wicked world," she cried, clapping her hands. "I'm just dying to know."

He looked at her, startled, remembering the wreckage of womanhood he had encountered on the sunken ways of life. She was no fairy. She was flesh and blood, and the possibilities of wreckage were in her as they had been in him even when he lay at his mother's breast. And there was in her eagerness to know.

"Nope," he said lightly, "this man from the bad, wicked world ain't going to tell you nothing of the kind. He's going to tell you of the good things in that world. He's going to tell you how he loved hosses when he was a shaver, and about the first hoss he straddled, and the first hoss he owned. Hosses ain't like men. They're better. They're clean—clean all the way through and back again. And, little fairy, I want to tell you one thing—there sure ain't nothing in the world like when you're settin' a tired hoss at the end of a long day, and when you just speak, and that tired animal lifts under you willing and hustles along. Hosses! They're my long suit. I sure dote on hosses. Yep. I used to be a cowboy once."

She clapped her hands in the way that tore so delightfully to his heart, and her eyes were dancing, as she exclaimed:

"A Texas cowboy! I always wanted to see one! I heard papa say once that cowboys are bow-legged. Are you?"

"I sure was a Texas cowboy," he answered. "But it was a long time ago. And I'm sure bow-legged. You see, you can't ride much when you're young and soft without getting the legs bent some. Why, I was only a three-year-old when I begun. He was a three-year-old, too, fresh-broken. I led him up alongside the fence, clumb to the top rail, and dropped on. He was a pinto, and a real devil at bucking, but I could do anything with him. I reckon he knowed I was only a little shaver. Some hosses knows lots more 'n' you think."

For half an hour Ross Shanklin rambled on with his horse reminiscences, never unconscious for a moment of the supreme joy that was his through the touch of his hand on the hem of her dress. The sun dropped slowly into the cloud bank, the quail called more insistently, and empty wagon after empty wagon rumbled back across the bridge. Then came a woman's voice.

"Joan! Joan!" it called. "Where are you, dear?"

The little girl answered, and Ross Shanklin saw a woman, clad in a soft, clinging gown, come through the gate from the bungalow. She was a slender, graceful woman, and to his charmed eyes she seemed rather to float along than walk like ordinary flesh and blood.

"What have you been doing all afternoon?" the woman asked, as she came up.

"Talking, mamma," the little girl replied "I've had a very interesting time."

Ross Shanklin scrambled to his feet and stood watchfully and awkwardly. The little girl took the mother's hand, and she, in turn, looked at him frankly and pleasantly, with a recognition of his humanness that was a new thing to him. In his mind ran the thought: *the woman who ain't afraid.* Not a hint was there of the timidity he was accustomed to seeing in women's eyes. And he was quite aware, and never more so, of his bleary-eyed, forbidding appearance.

"How do you do?" she greeted him sweetly and naturally.

"How do you do, ma'am," he responded, unpleasantly conscious of the huskiness and rawness of his voice.

"And did you have an interesting time, too?" she smiled.

"Yes, ma'am. I sure did. I was just telling your little girl about hosses."

"He was a cowboy, once, mamma," she cried.

The mother smiled her acknowledgment to him, and looked fondly down at the little girl. The thought that came into Ross Shanklin's mind was the awfulness of the crime if any one should harm either of the wonderful pair. This was followed by the wish that some terrible danger should threaten, so that he could fight, as he well knew how, with all his strength and life, to defend them.

"You'll have to come along, dear," the mother said. "It's growing late." She looked at Ross Shanklin hesitantly. "Would you care to have something to eat?"

"No, ma'am, thanking you kindly just the same. I ... I ain't hungry."

"Then say good-bye, Joan," she counselled.

"Good-bye." The little girl held out her hand, and her eyes lighted roguishly. "Good-bye, Mr. Man from the bad, wicked world."

To him, the touch of her hand as he pressed it in his was the capstone of the whole adventure.

"Good-bye, little fairy," he mumbled. "I reckon I got to be pullin' along."

But he did not pull along. He stood staring after his vision until it vanished through the gate. The day seemed suddenly empty. He looked about him irresolutely, then climbed the fence, crossed the bridge, and slouched along the road. He was in a dream. He did not note his feet nor the way they led him. At times he stumbled in the dust-filled ruts.

A mile farther on, he aroused at the crossroads. Before him stood the saloon. He came to a stop and stared at it, licking his lips. He sank his hand into his pants pocket and fumbled a solitary dime. "God!" he muttered. "God!" Then, with dragging, reluctant feet, went on along the road.

He came to a big farm. He knew it must be big, because of the bigness of the house and the size and number of the barns and outbuildings. On the porch, in shirt sleeves, smoking a cigar, keen-eyed and middle-aged, was the farmer.

"What's the chance for a job?" Ross Shanklin asked.

The keen eyes scarcely glanced at him.

"A dollar a day and grub," was the answer.

Ross Shanklin swallowed and braced himself.

"I'll pick grapes all right, or anything. But what's the chance for a steady job? You've got a big ranch here. I know hosses. I was born on one. I can drive team, ride, plough, break, do anything that anybody ever done with hosses."

The other looked him over with an appraising, incredulous eye.

"You don't look it," was the judgment.

"I know I don't. Give me a chance. That's all. I'll prove it."

The farmer considered, casting an anxious glance at the cloud bank into which the sun had sunk.

"I'm short a teamster, and I'll give you the chance to make good. Go and get supper with the hands."

Ross Shanklin's voice was very husky, and be spoke with an effort.

"All right. I'll make good. Where can I get a drink of water and wash up?'

THE PRODIGAL FATHER

I

Josiah Childs was ordinarily an ordinary-appearing, prosperous business man. He wore a sixty-dollar, business-man's suit, his shoes were comfortable and seemly and made from the current last, his tie, collars and cuffs were just what all prosperous business men wore, and an up-to-date, business-man's derby was his wildest adventure in head-gear. Oakland, California, is no sleepy country town, and Josiah Childs, as the leading grocer of a rushing Western metropolis of three hundred thousand, appropriately lived, acted, and dressed the part.

But on this morning, before the rush of custom began, his appearance at the store, while it did not cause a riot, was sufficiently startling to impair for half an hour the staff's working efficiency. He nodded pleasantly to the two delivery drivers loading their wagons for the first trip of the morning, and cast upward the inevitable, complacent glance at the sign that ran across the front of the building—CHILDS' CASH STORE. The lettering, not too large, was of dignified black and gold, suggestive of noble spices, aristocratic condiments, and everything of the best (which was no more than to be expected of a scale of prices ten per cent. higher than any other grocery in town). But what Josiah Childs did not see as he turned his back on the drivers and entered, was the helpless and mutual fall of surprise those two worthies perpetrated on each other's necks. They clung together for support.

"Did you catch the kicks, Bill?" one moaned.

"Did you pipe the head-piece?" Bill moaned back.

"Now if he was goin' to a masquerade ball...."

"Or attendin' a reunion of the Rough Riders...."

"Or goin' huntin' bear...."

"Or swearin' off his taxes...."

"Instead of goin' all the way to the effete East—Monkton says he's going clear to Boston...."

The two drivers held each other apart at arm's length, and fell limply together again.

For Josiah Childs' outfit was all their actions connotated. His hat was a light fawn, stiff-rimmed John B. Stetson, circled by a band of Mexican stamped leather. Over a blue flannel shirt, set off by a drooping Windsor tie, was a rough-and-ready coat of large-ribbed corduroy. Pants of the same material were thrust into high-laced shoes of the sort worn by surveyors, explorers, and linemen.

A clerk at a near counter almost petrified at sight of his employer's bizarre rig. Monkton, recently elevated to the managership. gasped, swallowed, and maintained his imperturbable attentiveness. The lady bookkeeper, glancing down from her glass eyrie on the inside balcony, took one look and buried her giggles in the day book. Josiah Childs saw most of all this, but he did not mind. He was starting on his vacation, and his head and heart were buzzing with plans and anticipations of the most adventurous vacation he had taken in ten years. Under his eyelids burned visions of East Falls, Connecticut, and of all the home scenes he had been born to and brought up in. Oakland, he was thoroughly aware, was more modern than East Falls, and the excitement caused by his garb was only to be expected. Undisturbed by the sensation he knew he was creating among his employes, he moved about, accompanied by his manager, making last suggestions, giving final instructions, and radiating fond, farewell glances at all the loved details of the business he had built out of nothing.

He had a right to be proud of Childs' Cash Store. Twelve years before he had landed in Oakland with fourteen dollars and forty-three cents. Cents did not circulate so far West, and after the fourteen dollars were gone, he continued to carry the three pennies in his pocket for a weary while. Later, when he had got a job clerking in a small grocery for eleven dollars a week, and had begun sending a small monthly postal order to one, Agatha Childs, East Falls, Connecticut, he invested the three coppers in postage stamps. Uncle Sam could not reject his own lawful coin of the realm.

Having spent all his life in cramped New England, where sharpness and shrewdness had been whetted to razor-edge on the harsh stone of meagre circumstance, he had found himself abruptly in the loose and free-and-easy West, where men thought in thousand-dollar bills and newsboys dropped dead at sight of copper cents. Josiah Childs bit like fresh acid into the new industrial and business conditions. He had vision. He saw so many ways of making money all at once, that at first his brain was in a whirl.

At the same time, being sane and conservative, he had resolutely avoided speculation. The solid and substantial called to him. Clerking at eleven dollars a week, he took note of the lost opportunities, of the openings for safe enterprise, of the countless leaks in the business. If, despite all this, the boss could make a good living, what couldn't he, Josiah Childs, do with his Connecticut training? It was like a bottle of wine to a thirsty hermit, this coming to the active, generous-spending West after thirty-five years in East Falls, the last fifteen of which had been spent in humdrum clerking in the humdrum East Falls general store. Josiah Childs' head buzzed with the easy possibilities he saw. But he did not lose his head. No detail was overlooked. He spent his spare hours in studying Oakland, its people, how they made their money, and why they spent it and where. He walked the central streets, watching the drift of the buying crowds, even counting them and compiling the statistics in various notebooks. He studied the general credit system of the trade, and the particular credit systems of the different districts. He could tell to a dot the average wage or salary earned by the householders of any locality, and he made it a point of thoroughness to know every locality from the waterfront slums to the aristocratic Lake Merritt and Piedmont sections, from West Oakland, where dwelt the railroad employes, to the semi-farmers of Fruitvale at the opposite end of the city.

Broadway, on the main street and in the very heart of the shopping district, where no grocer had ever been insane enough to dream of establishing a business, was his ultimate selection. But that required money, while he had to start from the smallest of beginnings. His first store was on lower Filbert, where lived the nail-workers. In half a year, three other little corner groceries went out of business while he was compelled to enlarge his premises. He understood the principle of large sales at small profits, of stable qualities of goods, and of a square deal. He had glimpsed, also, the secret of advertising. Each week he set forth one article that sold at a loss to him. This was not an advertised loss, but an absolute loss. His one clerk prophesied impending bankruptcy when butter, that cost Childs thirty cents, was sold for twenty-five cents, when twenty-two-cent coffee was passed across the counter at eighteen cents. The neighbourhood housewives came for these bargains and remained to buy other articles that sold at a profit. Moreover, the whole neighbourhood came quickly to know Josiah Childs, and the busy crowd of buyers in his store was an attraction in itself.

But Josiah Childs made no mistake. He knew the ultimate foundation on which his prosperity rested. He studied the nail works until he came to know as much about them as the managing directors. Before the first whisper had stirred abroad, he sold his store, and with a modest sum of ready cash went in search of a new location. Six months later the nail works closed down, and closed down forever.

His next store was established on Adeline Street, where lived a comfortable, salaried class. Here, his shelves carried a higher-grade and a more diversified stock. By the same old method, he drew his crowd. He established a delicatessen counter. He dealt directly with the farmers, so that his butter and eggs were not only always dependable but were a shade better than those sold by the finest groceries in the city. One of his specialties was Boston baked beans, and so popular did it become that the Twin Cabin Bakery paid him better than handsomely for the privilege of taking it over. He made time to study the farmers, the very apples they grew, and certain farmers he taught how properly to make cider. As a side-line, his New England apple cider proved his greatest success, and before long, after he had invaded San Francisco, Berkeley, and Alameda, he ran it as an independent business.

But always his eyes were fixed on Broadway. Only one other intermediate move did he make, which was to as near as he could get to the Ashland Park Tract, where every purchaser of land was legally pledged to put up no home that should cost less than four thousand dollars. After that came Broadway. A strange swirl had come in the tide of the crowd. The drift was to Washington Street, where real estate promptly soared while on Broadway it was as if the bottom had fallen out. One big store after another, as the leases expired, moved to Washington.

The crowd will come back, Josiah Childs said, but he said it to himself. He knew the crowd. Oakland was growing, and he knew why it was growing. Washington Street was too narrow to carry the increasing traffic. Along Broadway, in the physical nature of things, the electric cars, ever in greater numbers, would have to run. The realty dealers said that the crowd would never come back, while the leading merchants followed the crowd. And then it was, at a ridiculously low figure, that

Josiah Childs got a long lease on a modern, Class A building on Broadway with a buying option at a fixed price. It was the beginning of the end for Broadway, said the realty dealers, when a grocery was established in its erstwhile sacred midst. Later, when the crowd did come back, they said Josiah Childs was lucky. Also, they whispered among themselves that he had cleared at least fifty thousand on the transaction.

It was an entirely different store from his previous ones. There were no more bargains. Everything was of the superlative best, and superlative best prices were charged. He catered to the most expensive trade in town. Only those who could carelessly afford to pay ten per cent. more than anywhere else, patronised him, and so excellent was his service that they could not afford to go elsewhere. His horses and delivery wagons were more expensive and finer than any one else's in town. He paid his drivers, and clerks, and bookkeepers higher wages than any other store could dream of paying. As a result, he got more efficient men, and they rendered him and his patrons a more satisfying service. In short, to deal at Childs' Cash Store became almost the infallible index of social status.

To cap everything, came the great San Francisco earthquake and fire, which caused one hundred thousand people abruptly to come across the Bay and live in Oakland. Not least to profit from so extraordinary a boom, was Josiah Childs. And now, after twelve years' absence, he was departing on a visit to East Falls, Connecticut. In the twelve years he had not received a letter from Agatha, nor had he seen even a photograph of his and Agatha's boy.

Agatha and he had never got along together. Agatha was masterful. Agatha had a tongue. She was strong on old-fashioned morality. She was unlovely in her rectitude. Josiah never could quite make out how he had happened to marry her. She was two years his senior, and had long ranked as an old maid She had taught school, and was known by the young generation as the sternest disciplinarian in its experience. She had become set in her ways, and when she married it was merely an exchange of a number of pupils for one. Josiah had to stand the hectoring and nagging that thitherto had been distributed among many. As to how the marriage came about, his Uncle Isaac nearly hit it off one day when he said in confidence: "Josiah, when Agatha married you it was a case of marrying a struggling young man. I reckon you was overpowered. Or maybe you broke your leg and couldn't get away."

"Uncle Isaac," Josiah answered, "I didn't break my leg. I ran my dangdest, but she just plum run me down and out of breath."

"Strong in the wind, eh?" Uncle Isaac chuckled.

"We've ben married five years now," Josiah agreed, "and I've never known her to lose it."

"And never will," Uncle Isaac added.

This conversation had taken place in the last days, and so dismal an outlook proved too much for Josiah Childs. Meek he was, under Agatha's firm tuition, but he was very healthy, and his promise of life was too long for his patience. He was only thirty-three, and he came of a long-lived stock. Thirty-three more years with Agatha and Agatha's nagging was too hideous to contemplate. So, between a sunset and a rising, Josiah Childs disappeared from East Falls. And from that day, for twelve years, he had received no letter from her. Not that it was her fault. He had carefully avoided letting her have his address. His first postal money orders were sent to her from Oakland, but in the years that followed he had arranged his remittances so that they bore the scattered postmarks of most of the states west of the Rockies.

But twelve years, and the confidence born of deserved success, had softened his memories. After all, she was the mother of his boy, and it was incontestable that she had always meant well. Besides, he was not working so hard now, and he had more time to think of things besides his business. He wanted to see the boy, whom he had never seen and who had turned three before his father ever learned he was a father. Then, too, homesickness had begun to crawl in him. In a dozen years he had not seen snow, and he was always wondering if New England fruits and berries had not a finer tang than those of California. Through hazy vistas he saw the old New England life, and he wanted to see it again in the flesh before he died.

And, finally, there was duty. Agatha was his wife. He would bring her back with him to the West. He felt that he could stand it. He was a man, now, in the world of men. He ran things, instead of being run, and Agatha would quickly find it out. Nevertheless, he wanted Agatha to come to him for his own sake. So it was that he had put on his frontier rig. He would be the prodigal father, returning as penniless as when he left, and it would be up to her whether or not she killed the fatted calf. Empty of hand, and looking it, he would come back wondering if he could get his old job in the general store. Whatever followed would be Agatha's affair.

By the time he said good-bye to his staff and emerged on the sidewalk, five more of his delivery wagons were backed up and loading.

He ran his eye proudly over them, took a last fond glance at the black-and-gold letters, and signalled the electric car at the corner.

II

He ran up to East Falls from New York. In the Pullman smoker he became acquainted with several business men. The conversation, turning on the West, was quickly led by him. As president of the Oakland Chamber of Commerce, he was an authority. His words carried weight, and he knew what he was talking about, whether it was Asiatic trade, the Panama Canal, or the Japanese coolie question. It was very exhilarating, this stimulus of respectful attention accorded him by these prosperous Eastern men, and before he knew it he was at East Falls.

He was the only person who alighted, and the station was deserted. Nobody was there expecting anybody. The long twilight of a January evening was beginning, and the bite of the keen air made him suddenly conscious that his clothing was saturated with tobacco smoke. He shuddered involuntarily. Agatha did not tolerate tobacco. He half-moved to toss the fresh-lighted cigar away, then it was borne in upon him that this was the old East Falls atmosphere overpowering him, and he resolved to combat it, thrusting the cigar between his teeth and gripping it with the firmness of a dozen years of Western resolution.

A few steps brought him into the little main street. The chilly, stilted aspect of it shocked him. Everything seemed frosty and pinched, just as the cutting air did after the warm balminess of California. Only several persons, strangers to his recollection, were abroad, and they favoured him with incurious glances. They were wrapped in an uncongenial and frosty imperviousness. His first impression was surprise at his surprise. Through the wide perspective of twelve years of Western life, he had consistently and steadily discounted the size and importance of East Falls; but this was worse than all discounting. Things were more meagre than he had dreamed. The general store took his breath away. Countless myriads of times he had contrasted it with his own spacious emporium, but now he saw that in justice he had overdone it. He felt certain that it could not accommodate two of his delicatessen counters, and he knew that he could lose all of it in one of his storerooms.

He took the familiar turning to the right at the head of the street, and as he plodded along the slippery walk he decided that one of the first things he must do was to buy sealskin cap and gloves. The thought of sleighing cheered him for a moment, until, now on the outskirts of the village, he was sanitarily perturbed by the adjacency of dwelling houses and barns. Some were even connected. Cruel memories of bitter morning chores oppressed him. The thought of chapped hands and chilblains was almost terrifying, and his heart sank at sight of the double storm-windows, which he knew were solidly fastened and unraisable, while the small ventilating panes, the size of ladies' handkerchiefs, smote him with sensations of suffocation. Agatha'll like California, he thought, calling to his mind visions of roses in dazzling sunshine and the wealth of flowers that bloomed the twelve months round.

And then, quite illogically, the years were bridged and the whole leaden weight of East Falls descended upon him like a damp sea fog. He fought it from him, thrusting it off and aside by sentimental thoughts on the "honest snow," the "fine elms," the "sturdy New England spirit," and the "great home-coming." But at sight of Agatha's house he wilted. Before he knew it, with a recrudescent guilty pang, he had tossed the half-smoked cigar away and slackened his pace until his feet dragged in the old lifeless, East Falls manner. He tried to remember that he was the owner of Childs' Cash Store, accustomed to command, whose words were listened to with respect in the Employers' Association, and who wielded the gavel at the meetings of the Chamber of Commerce. He strove to conjure visions of the letters in black and gold, and of the string of delivery wagons backed up to the sidewalk. But Agatha's New England spirit was as sharp as the frost, and it travelled to him through solid house-walls and across the intervening hundred yards.

Then he became aware that despite his will he had thrown the cigar away. This brought him an awful vision. He saw himself going out in the frost to the woodshed to smoke. His memory of Agatha he found less softened by the lapse of years than it had been when three thousand miles intervened. It was unthinkable. No; he couldn't do it. He was too old, too used to smoking all over the house, to do the woodshed stunt now. And everything depended on how he began. He would put his foot down. He would smoke in the house that very night ... in the kitchen, he feebly amended. No, by George, he would smoke now. He would arrive smoking. Mentally imprecating the cold, he exposed his bare hands and lighted another cigar. His manhood seemed to flare up with the match. He would show her who was boss. Right from the drop of the hat he would show her.

Josiah Childs had been born in this house. And it was long before he was born that his father had built it. Across the low stone fence, Josiah could see the kitchen porch and door, the connected woodshed, and the several outbuildings. Fresh from the West, where everything was new and in constant flux, he was astonished at the lack of change. Everything was as it had always been. He could almost see himself, a boy, doing the chores. There, in the woodshed, how many cords of wood had he bucksawed and split! Well, thank the Lord, that was past.

The walk to the kitchen showed signs of recent snow-shovelling. That had been one of his tasks. He wondered who did it now, and suddenly remembered that his own son must be twelve. In another moment he would have knocked at the kitchen door, but the *skreek* of a bucksaw from the woodshed led him aside. He looked in and saw a boy hard at work. Evidently, this was his son. Impelled by the wave of warm emotion that swept over him, he all but rushed in upon the lad. He controlled himself with an effort.

"Father here?" he asked curtly, though from under the stiff brim of his John B. Stetson he studied the boy closely.

Sizable for his age, he thought. A mite spare in the ribs maybe, and that possibly due to rapid growth. But the face strong and pleasing and the eyes like Uncle Isaac's. When all was said, a darn good sample.

"No, sir," the boy answered, resting on the saw-buck.

"Where is he?"

"At sea," was the answer.

Josiah Childs felt a something very akin to relief and joy tingle through him. Agatha had married again—evidently a seafaring man. Next, came an ominous, creepy sensation. Agatha had committed bigamy. He remembered Enoch Arden, read aloud to the class by the teacher in the old schoolhouse, and began to think of himself as a hero. He would do the heroic. By George, he would. He would sneak away and get the first train for California. She would never know.

But there was Agatha's New England morality, and her New England conscience. She received a regular remittance. She knew he was alive. It was impossible that she could have done this thing. He groped wildly for a solution. Perhaps she had sold the old home, and this boy was somebody else's boy.

"What is your name?" Josiah asked.

"Johnnie," came the reply.

"Last name I mean?"

"Childs, Johnnie Childs."

"And your father's name?—first name?"

"Josiah Childs."

"And he's away at sea, you say?"

"Yes, sir."

This set Josiah wondering again.

"What kind of a man is he?"

"Oh, he's all right—a good provider, Mom says. And he is. He always sends his money home, and he works hard for it, too, Mom says. She says he always was a good worker, and he's better'n other men she ever saw. He don't smoke, or drink, or swear, or do anything he oughtn't. And he never did. He was always that way, Mom says, and she knew him all her life before ever they got married. He's a very kind man, and never hurts anybody's feelings. Mom says he's the most considerate man she ever knew."

Josiah's heart went weak. Agatha had done it after all—had taken a second husband when she knew her first was still alive. Well, he had learned charity in the West, and he could be charitable. He would go quietly away. Nobody would ever know. Though it was rather mean of her, the thought flashed through him, that she should go on cashing his remittances when she was married to so model and steady-working a seafaring husband who brought his wages home. He cudgelled his brains in an effort to remember such a man out of all the East Falls men he had known.

"What's he look like?"

"Don't know. Never saw him. He's at sea all the time. But I know how tall he is. Mom says I'm goin' to be bigger'n him, and he was five feet eleven. There's a picture of him in the album. His face is thin, and he has whiskers."

A great illumination came to Josiah. He was himself five feet eleven. He had worn whiskers, and his face had been thin in those days. And Johnnie had said his father's name was Josiah Childs. He, Josiah, was this model husband who neither smoked, swore, nor drank. He was this seafaring man whose memory had been so carefully shielded by Agatha's forgiving fiction. He warmed toward her. She must have changed mightily since he left. He glowed with penitence. Then his heart sank as he thought of trying to live up to this reputation Agatha had made for him. This boy with the trusting blue eyes would expect it of him. Well, he'd have to do it. Agatha had been almighty square with him. He hadn't thought she had it in her.

The resolve he might there and then have taken was doomed never to be, for he heard the kitchen door open to give vent to a woman's nagging, irritable voice.

"Johnnie!—you!" it cried.

How often had he heard it in the old days: "Josiah!—you!" A shiver went through him. Involuntarily, automatically, with a guilty start, he turned his hand back upward so that the cigar was hidden. He felt himself shrinking and shrivelling as she stepped out on the stoop. It was his unchanged wife, the same shrew wrinkles, with the same sour-drooping corners to the thin-lipped mouth. But there was more sourness, an added droop, the lips were thinner, and the shrew wrinkles were deeper. She swept Josiah with a hostile, withering stare.

"Do you think your father would stop work to talk to tramps?" she demanded of the boy, who visibly quailed, even as Josiah.

"I was only answering his questions," Johnnie pleaded doggedly but hopelessly. "He wanted to know—"

"And I suppose you told him," she snapped. "What business is it of his prying around? No, and he gets nothing to eat. As for you, get to work at once. I'll teach you, idling at your chores. Your father wa'n't like that. Can't I ever make you like him?"

Johnnie bent his back, and the bucksaw resumed its protesting skreek. Agatha surveyed Josiah sourly. It was patent she did not recognise him.

"You be off," she commanded harshly. "None of your snooping around here."

Josiah felt the numbness of paralysis creeping over him. He moistened his lips and tried to say something, but found himself bereft of speech.

"You be off, I say," she rasped in her high-keyed voice, "or I'll put the constable after you."

Josiah turned obediently. He heard the door slam as he went down the walk. As in a nightmare he opened the gate he had opened ten thousand times and stepped out on the sidewalk. He felt dazed. Surely it was a dream. Very soon he would wake up with a sigh of relief. He rubbed his forehead and paused indecisively. The monotonous complaint of the bucksaw came to his ears. If that boy had any of the old Childs spirit in him, sooner or later he'd run away. Agatha was beyond the endurance of human flesh. She had not changed, unless for the worse, if such a thing were possible. That boy would surely run for it, maybe soon. Maybe now.

Josiah Childs straightened up and threw his shoulders back. The great-spirited West, with its daring and its carelessness of consequences when mere obstacles stand in the way of its desire, flamed up in him. He looked at his watch, remembered the time table, and spoke to himself, solemnly, aloud. It was an affirmation of faith:

"I don't care a hang about the law. That boy can't be crucified. I'll give her a double allowance, four times, anything, but he goes with me. She can follow on to California if she wants, but I'll draw up an agreement, in which what's what, and she'll sign it, and live up to it, by George, if she wants to stay. And she will," he added grimly. "She's got to have somebody to nag."

He opened the gate and strode back to the woodshed door. Johnnie looked up, but kept on sawing.

"What'd you like to do most of anything in the world?" Josiah demanded in a tense, low voice.

Johnnie hesitated, and almost stopped sawing. Josiah made signs for him to keep it up.

"Go to sea," Johnnie answered. "Along with my father."

Josiah felt himself trembling.

"Would you?" he asked eagerly.

"Would I!"

The look of joy on Johnnie's face decided everything.

"Come here, then. Listen. I'm your father. I'm Josiah Childs. Did you ever want to run away?"

Johnnie nodded emphatically.

"That's what I did," Josiah went on. "I ran away." He fumbled for his watch hurriedly. "We've just time to catch the train for California. I live there now. Maybe Agatha, your mother, will come along afterward. I'll tell you all about it on the train. Come on."

He gathered the half-frightened, half-trusting boy into his arms for a moment, then, hand in hand, they fled across the yard, out of the gate, and down the street. They heard the kitchen door open, and the last they heard was:

"Johnnie!—you! Why ain't you sawing? I'll attend to your case directly!"

THE FIRST POET

SCENE: *A summer plain, the eastern side of which is bounded by grassy hills of limestone, the other sides by a forest. The hill nearest to the plain terminates in a cliff, in the face of which, nearly at the level of the ground, are four caves, with low, narrow entrances. Before the caves, and distant from them less than one hundred feet, is a broad, flat rock, on which are laid several sharp slivers of flint, which, like the rock, are blood-stained. Between the rock and the cave-entrances, on a low pile of stones, is squatted a man, stout and hairy. Across his knees is a thick club, and behind him crouches a woman. At his right and left are two men somewhat resembling him, and like him, bearing wooden clubs. These four face the west, and between them and the bloody rock squat some threescore of cave-folk, talking loudly among themselves. It is late afternoon. The name of him on the pile of stones is Uk, the name of his mate, Ala; and of those at his right and left, Ok and Un.*

Uk:

Be still!

(*Turning to the woman behind him*)

Thou seest that they become still. None save me can make his kind be still, except perhaps the chief of the apes, when in the night he deems he hears a serpent.... At whom dost thou stare so long? At Oan? Oan, come to me!

Oan:

I am thy cub.

Uk:

Oan, thou art a fool!

Ok and Un:

Ho! ho! Oan is a fool!

All the Tribe:

Ho! ho! Oan is a fool!

Oan:

Why am I a fool?

Uk:

Dost thou not chant strange words? Last night I heard thee chant strange words at the mouth of thy cave.

Oan:

Ay! they are marvellous words; they were born within me in the dark.

Uk:

Art thou a woman, that thou shouldst bring forth? Why dost thou not sleep when it is dark?

Oan:

I did half sleep; perhaps I dreamed.

Uk:

And why shouldst thou dream, not having had more than thy portion of flesh? Hast thou slain a deer in the forest and brought it not to the Stone?

All the Tribe:

Wa! Wa! He hath slain in the forest, and brought not the meat to the Stone!

Uk:

Be still, ye!

(*To Ala*)

Thou seest that they become still.... Oan, hast thou slain and kept to thyself?

Oan:

Nay, thou knowest that I am not apt at the chase. Also it irks me to squat on a branch all day above a path, bearing a rock upon my thighs. Those words did but awaken within me when I was peaceless in the night.

Uk:

And why wast thou peaceless in the night?

Oan:

Thy mate wept, for that thou didst heat her.

Uk:

Ay! she lamented loudly. But thou shalt make thy half-sleep henceforth at the mouth of the cave, so that when Gurr the tiger cometh, thou shalt hear him sniff between the boulders, and shalt strike the flints, whose stare he hatest. Gurr cometh nightly to the caves.

One of the Tribe:

Ay! Gurr smelleth the Stone!

Uk:

Be still!

(*To Ala*)

Had he not become still, Ok and Un would have beaten him with their clubs.... But, Oan, tell us those words that were born to thee when Ala did weep.

Oan (arising):

They are wonderful words. They are such:

  The bright day is gone—

Uk:

Now I see thou art liar as well as fool: behold, the day is not gone!

Oan:

But the day was gone in that hour when my song was born to me.

Uk:

Then shouldst thou have sung it only at that time, and not when it is yet day. But beware lest thou awaken me in the night. Make thou many stars, that they fly in the whiskers of Gurr.

Oan:

My song is even of stars.

Uk:

It was Ul, thy father's wont, ere I slew him with four great stones, to climb to the tops of the tallest trees and reach forth his hand, to see if he might not pluck a star. But I said: "Perhaps they be as chestnut-burs." And all the tribe did laugh. Ul was also a fool. But what dost thou sing of stars?

Oan:

I will begin again:

> The bright day is gone.
> The night maketh me sad, sad, sad—

Uk:

Nay, the night maketh thee sad; not sad, sad, sad. For when I say to Ala, "Gather thou dried leaves," I say not, "Gather thou dried leaves, leaves, leaves." Thou art a fool!

Ok and Un:

Thou art a fool!

All the Tribe:

Thou art a fool!

Uk:

Yea, he is a fool. But say on, Oan, and tell us of thy chestnut-burs.

Oan:

I will begin again:

The bright day is gone—

Uk:

Thou dost not say, "gone, gone, gone!"

Oan:

I am thy cub. Suffer that I speak: so shall the tribe admire greatly.

Uk:

Speak on!

Oan:

I will begin once more:

The bright day is gone.
The night maketh me sad, sad—

Uk:

Said I not that "sad" should be spoken but once? Shall I set Ok and Un upon thee with their branches?

Oan:

But it was so born within me—even "sad, sad—"

Uk:

If again thou twice or thrice say "sad," thou shalt be dragged to the Stone.

Oan:

Owl Ow! I am thy cub! Yet listen:

> The bright day is gone.
> The night maketh me sad—

Ow! Ow! thou makest me more sad than the night doth! The song—

Uk:

Ok! Un! Be prepared!

Oan (hastily):

Nay! have mercy! I will begin afresh:

> The bright day is gone.
> The night maketh me sad.
> The—the—the—

Uk:

Thou hast forgotten, and art a fool! See, Ala, he is a fool!

Ok and Un:

He is a fool!

All the Tribe:

He is a fool!

Oan:

I am not a fool! This is a new thing. In the past, when ye did chant, O men, ye did leap about the Stone, beating your breasts and crying, "Hai, hai, hai!" Or, if the moon was great, "Hai, hai! hai, hai, hai!" But this song is made even with such words as ye do speak, and is a great wonder. One may sit at the cave's mouth, and moan it many times as the light goeth out of the sky.

One of the Tribe:

Ay! even thus doth he sit at the mouth of our cave, making us marvel, and more especially the women.

Uk:

Be still!... When I would make women marvel, I do show them a wolf's brains upon my club, or the great stone that I cast, or perhaps do whirl my arms mightily, or bring home much meat. How should a man do otherwise? I will have no songs in this place.

Oan:

Yet suffer that I sing my song unto the tribe. Such things have not been before. It may be that they shall praise thee, seeing that I who do make this song am thy cub.

Uk:

Well, let us have the song.

Oan (facing the tribe):

> The bright day is gone.
> The night maketh me sa—sad.
> But the stars are very white.
> They whisper that the day shall return.
> O stars; little pieces of the day!

Uk:

This is indeed madness. Hast thou heard a star whisper? Did Ul, thy father, tell thee that he heard the stars whisper when he was in the tree-top? And of what moment is it that a star be a piece of the day, seeing that its light is of no value? Thou art a fool!

Ok and Un:

Thou art a fool!

All the Tribe:

Thou art a fool!

Oan:

But it was so born unto me. And at that birth it was as though I would weep, yet had not been stricken; I was moreover glad, yet none had given me a gift of meat.

Uk:

It is a madness. How shall the stars profit us? Will they lead us to a bear's den, or where the deer foregather, or break for us great bones that we come at their marrow? Will they tell us anything at all? Wait thou until the night, and we shall peer forth from between the boulders, and all men shall take note that the stars cannot whisper.... Yet it may be that they are pieces of the day. This is a deep matter.

Oan:

Ay! they are pieces of the moon!

Uk:

What further madness is this? How shall they be pieces of two things that are not the same? Also it was not thus in the song.

Oan:

I will make me a new song. We do change the shape of wood

and stone, but a song is made out of nothing. Ho! ho! I can fashion things from nothing! Also I say that the stars come down at morning and become the dew.

Uk:

Let us have no more of these stars. It may be that a song is a good thing, if it be of what a man knoweth. Thus, if thou singest of my club, or of the bear that I slew, of the stain on the Stone, or the cave and the warm leaves in the cave, it might be well.

Oan:

I will make thee a song of Ala!

Uk (furiously):

Thou shalt make me no such song! Thou shalt make me a song of the deer-liver that thou hast eaten! Did I not give to thee of the liver of the she-deer, because thou didst bring me crawfish?

Oan:

Truly I did eat of the liver of the she-deer; but to sing thereof is another matter.

Uk:

It was no labour for thee to sing of the stars. See now our clubs and casting-stones, with which we slay flesh to eat; also the caves in which we dwell, and the Stone whereon we make sacrifice; wilt thou sing no song of those?

Oan:

It may be that I shall sing thee songs of them. But now, as I strive here to sing of the doe's liver, no words are born unto me: I can but sing, "O liver! O red liver!"

Uk:

That is a good song: thou seest that the liver is red. It is red as blood.

Oan:

But I love not the liver, save to eat of it.

Uk:

Yet the song of it is good. When the moon is full we shall sing it about the Stone. We shall beat upon our breasts and sing, "O liver! O red liver!" And all the women in the caves shall be affrightened.

Oan:

I will not have that song of the liver! It shall be Ok's song; the tribe must say, "Ok hath made the song!"

Ok:

Ay! I shall be a great singer; I shall sing of a wolf's heart, and say, "Behold, it is red!"

Uk:

Thou art a fool, and shalt sing only, "Hai, hai!" as thy father before thee. But Oan shall make me a song of my club, for the women listen to his songs.

Oan:

I will make thee no songs, neither of thy club, nor thy cave, nor thy doe's-liver. Yea! though thou give me no more flesh, yet will I live alone in the forest, and eat the seed of grasses, and likewise rabbits, that are easily snared. And I will sleep in a tree-top, and I will sing nightly:

The bright day is gone.
The night maketh me sad, sad, sad,
sad, sad, sad—

Uk:

Ok and Un, arise and slay!

(*Ok and Un rush upon Oan, who stoops and picks up two casting-stones, with one of which he strikes Ok between the eyes, and with the other mashes the hand of Un, so that he drops his club. Uk arises.*)

Uk:

Behold! Gurr cometh! he cometh swiftly from the wood!

(*The Tribe, including Oan and Ala, rush for the cave-mouths. As Oan passes Uk, the latter runs behind Oan and crushes his skull with a blow of his club.*)

Uk:

O men! O men with the heart of hyenas! Behold, Gurr cometh not! I did but strive to deceive you, that I might the more easily slay this singer, who is very swift of foot.... Gather ye before me, for I would speak wisdom.... It is not well that there be any song among us other than what our fathers sang in the past, or, if there be songs, let them be of such matters as are of common understanding. If a man sing of a deer, so shall he be drawn, it may be, to go forth and slay a deer, or even a moose. And if he sing of his casting-stones, it may be that he become more apt in the use thereof. And if he sing of his cave, it may be that he shall defend it more stoutly when Gurr teareth at the boulders. But it is a vain thing to make songs of the stars, that seem scornful even of me; or of the moon, which is never two nights the same; or of the day, which goeth about its business and will not linger though one pierce a she-babe with a flint. But as for me, I would have none of these songs. For if

I sing of such in the council, how shall I keep my wits? And if I think thereof, when at the chase, it may be that I babble it forth, and the meat hear and escape. And ere it be time to eat, I do give my mind solely to the care of my hunting-gear. And if one sing when eating, he may fall short of his just portion. And when, one hath eaten, doth not he go straightway to sleep? So where shall men find a space for singing? But do ye as ye will: as for me, I will have none of these songs and stars.

Be it also known to all the women that if, remembering these wild words of Oan, they do sing them to themselves, or teach them to the young ones, they shall be beaten with brambles. Cause swiftly that the wife of Ok cease from her wailing, and bring hither the horses that were slain yesterday, that I may apportion them. Had Oan wisdom, he might have eaten thereof; and had a mammoth fallen into our pit, he might have feasted many days. But Oan was a fool!

Un:

Oan was a fool!

All the Tribe:

Oan was a fool!

FINIS

It was the last of Morganson's bacon. In all his life he had never pampered his stomach. In fact, his stomach had been a sort of negligible quantity that bothered him little, and about which he thought less. But now, in the long absence of wonted delights, the keen yearning of his stomach was tickled hugely by the sharp, salty bacon.

His face had a wistful, hungry expression. The cheeks were hollow, and the skin seemed stretched a trifle tightly across the cheek-bones. His pale blue eyes were troubled. There was that in them that showed the haunting imminence of something terrible. Doubt was in them, and anxiety and foreboding. The thin lips were thinner than they were made to be, and they seemed to hunger towards the polished frying-pan.

He sat back and drew forth a pipe. He looked into it with sharp scrutiny, and tapped it emptily on his open palm. He turned the hair-seal tobacco pouch inside out and dusted the lining, treasuring carefully each flake and mite of tobacco that his efforts gleaned. The result was scarce a thimbleful. He searched in his pockets, and brought forward, between thumb and forefinger, tiny pinches of rubbish. Here and there in this rubbish were crumbs of tobacco. These he segregated with microscopic care, though he occasionally permitted small particles of foreign substance to accompany the crumbs to the hoard in his palm. He even deliberately added small, semi-hard woolly fluffs, that had come originally from the coat lining, and that had lain for long months in the bottoms of the pockets.

At the end of fifteen minutes he had the pipe part filled. He lighted it from the camp fire, and sat forward on the blankets, toasting his moccasined feet and smoking parsimoniously. When the pipe was finished he sat on, brooding into the dying flame of the fire. Slowly the worry went out of his eyes and resolve came in. Out of the chaos of his fortunes he had finally achieved a way. But it was not a pretty way. His face had become stern and wolfish, and the thin lips were drawn very tightly.

With resolve came action. He pulled himself stiffly to his feet and proceeded to break camp. He packed the rolled blankets, the frying-pan, rifle, and axe on the sled, and passed a lashing around the load. Then he warmed his hands at the fire and pulled on his mittens. He was foot-sore, and limped noticeably as he took his place at the head of the sled. When he put the looped haul-rope over his shoulder, and leant his weight against it to start the sled, he winced. His flesh was galled by many days of contact with the haul-rope.

The trail led along the frozen breast of the Yukon. At the end of four hours he came around a bend and entered the town of Minto. It was perched on top of a high earth bank in the midst of a clearing, and consisted of a road house, a saloon, and several cabins. He left his sled at the door and entered the saloon.

"Enough for a drink?" he asked, laying an apparently empty gold sack upon the bar.

The barkeeper looked sharply at it and him, then set out a bottle and a glass.

"Never mind the dust," he said.

"Go on and take it," Morganson insisted.

The barkeeper held the sack mouth downward over the scales and shook it, and a few flakes of gold dust fell out. Morganson took the sack from him, turned it inside out, and dusted it carefully.

"I thought there was half-a-dollar in it," he said.

"Not quite," answered the other, "but near enough. I'll get it back with the down weight on the next comer."

Morganson shyly poured the whisky into the glass, partly filling it.

"Go on, make it a man's drink," the barkeeper encouraged.

Morganson tilted the bottle and filled the glass to the brim. He drank the liquor slowly, pleasuring in the fire of it that bit his tongue, sank hotly down his throat, and with warm, gentle caresses permeated his stomach.

"Scurvy, eh?" the barkeeper asked.

"A touch of it," he answered. "But I haven't begun to swell yet. Maybe I can get to Dyea and fresh vegetables, and beat it out."

"Kind of all in, I'd say," the other laughed sympathetically. "No dogs, no money, and the scurvy. I'd try spruce tea if I was you."

At the end of half-an-hour, Morganson said good-bye and left the saloon. He put his galled shoulder to the haul-rope and took the river-trail south. An hour later he halted. An inviting swale left the river and led off to the right at an acute angle. He left his sled and limped up the swale for half a mile. Between him and the river was three hundred yards of flat ground covered with cottonwoods. He crossed the cottonwoods to the bank of the Yukon. The trail went by just beneath, but he did not descend to it. South toward Selkirk he could see the trail widen its sunken length through the snow for over a mile. But to the north, in the direction of Minto, a tree-covered out-jut in the bank a quarter of a mile away screened the trail from him.

He seemed satisfied with the view and returned to the sled the way he had come. He put the haul-rope over his shoulder and dragged the sled up the swale. The snow was unpacked and soft, and it was hard work. The runners clogged and stuck, and he was panting severely ere he had covered the half-mile. Night had come on by the time he had pitched his small tent, set up the sheet-iron stove, and chopped a supply of firewood. He had no candles, and contented himself with a pot of tea before crawling into his blankets.

In the morning, as soon as he got up, he drew on his mittens, pulled the flaps of his cap down over his ears, and crossed through the cottonwoods to the Yukon. He took his rifle with him. As before, he did not descend the bank. He watched the empty trail for an hour, beating his hands and stamping his feet to keep up the circulation, then returned to the tent for breakfast. There was little tea left in the canister—half a dozen drawings at most; but so meagre a pinch did he put in the teapot that he bade fair to extend the lifetime of the tea indefinitely. His entire food supply consisted of half-a-sack of flour and a part-full can of baking powder. He made biscuits, and ate them slowly, chewing each mouthful with infinite relish. When he had had three he called a halt. He debated a while, reached for another biscuit, then hesitated. He turned to the part sack of flour, lifted it, and judged its weight.

"I'm good for a couple of weeks," he spoke aloud.

"Maybe three," he added, as he put the biscuits away.

Again he drew on his mittens, pulled down his ear-flaps, took the rifle, and went out to his station on the river bank. He crouched in the snow, himself unseen, and watched. After a few minutes of inaction, the frost began to bite in, and he rested the rifle across his knees and beat his hands back and forth. Then the sting in his feet became intolerable, and he stepped back from the bank and tramped heavily up and down among the trees. But he did not tramp long at a time. Every several minutes he came to the edge of the bank and peered up and down the trail, as though by sheer will he could materialise the form of a man upon it. The short morning passed, though it had seemed century-long to him, and the trail remained empty.

It was easier in the afternoon, watching by the bank. The temperature rose, and soon the snow began to fall—dry and fine and crystalline. There was no wind, and it fell straight down, in quiet monotony. He crouched with eyes closed, his head upon his knees, keeping his watch upon the trail with his ears. But no whining of dogs, churning of sleds, nor cries of drivers broke the silence. With twilight he returned to the tent, cut a supply of firewood, ate two biscuits, and crawled into his blankets. He slept restlessly, tossing about and groaning; and at midnight he got up and ate another biscuit.

Each day grew colder. Four biscuits could not keep up the heat of his body, despite the quantities of hot spruce tea he drank, and he increased his allowance, morning and evening, to three biscuits. In the middle of the day he ate nothing, contenting himself with several cups of excessively weak real tea. This programme became routine. In the morning three biscuits, at noon real tea, and at night three biscuits. In between he drank spruce tea for his scurvy. He caught himself making larger biscuits, and after a severe struggle with himself went back to the old size.

On the fifth day the trail returned to life. To the south a dark object appeared, and grew larger. Morganson became alert. He worked his rifle, ejecting a loaded cartridge from the chamber, by the same action replacing it with another, and returning the ejected cartridge into the magazine. He lowered the trigger to half-cock, and drew on his mitten to keep the trigger-hand warm. As the dark object came nearer he made it out to be a man, without dogs or sled, travelling light. He grew nervous, cocked the trigger, then put it back to half-cock again. The man developed into an Indian, and Morganson, with a sigh of disappointment, dropped the rifle across his knees. The Indian went on past and disappeared towards Minto behind the out-jutting clump of trees.

But Morganson conceived an idea. He changed his crouching spot to a place where cottonwood limbs projected on either side of him. Into these with his axe he chopped two broad notches. Then in one of the notches he rested the barrel of his rifle and glanced along the sights. He covered the trail thoroughly in that direction. He turned about, rested the rifle in the other notch, and, looking along the sights, swept the trail to the clump of trees behind which it disappeared.

He never descended to the trail. A man travelling the trail could have no knowledge of his lurking presence on the bank above. The snow surface was unbroken. There was no place where his tracks left the main trail.

As the nights grew longer, his periods of daylight watching of the trail grew shorter. Once a sled went by with jingling bells in the darkness, and with sullen resentment he chewed his biscuits and listened to the sounds. Chance conspired against him. Faithfully he had watched the trail for ten days, suffering from the cold all the prolonged torment of the damned, and nothing had happened. Only an Indian, travelling light, had passed in. Now, in the night, when it was impossible for him to watch, men and dogs and a sled loaded with life, passed out, bound south to the sea and the sun and civilisation.

So it was that he conceived of the sled for which he waited. It was loaded with life, his life. His life was fading, fainting, gasping away in the tent in the snow. He was weak from lack of food, and could not travel of himself. But on the sled for which he waited were dogs that would drag him, food that would fan up the flame of his life, money that would furnish sea and sun and civilisation. Sea and sun and civilization became terms interchangeable with life, his life, and they were loaded there on the sled for which he waited. The idea became an obsession, and he grew to think of himself as the rightful and deprived owner of the sled-load of life.

His flour was running short, and he went back to two biscuits in the morning and two biscuits at night. Because, of this his weakness increased and the cold bit in more savagely, and day by day he watched by the dead trail that would not live for him. At last the scurvy entered upon its next stage. The skin was unable longer to cast off the impurity of the blood, and the result was that the body began to swell. His ankles grew puffy, and the ache in them kept him awake long hours at night. Next, the swelling jumped to his knees, and the sum of his pain was more than doubled.

Then there came a cold snap. The temperature went down and down—forty, fifty, sixty degrees below zero. He had no thermometer, but this he knew by the signs and natural phenomena understood by all men in that country—the crackling of water thrown on the snow, the swift sharpness of the bite of the frost, and the rapidity with which his breath froze and coated the canvas walls and roof of the tent. Vainly he fought the cold and strove to maintain his watch on the bank. In his weak condition he was an easy prey, and the frost sank its teeth deep into him before he fled away to the tent and crouched by the fire. His nose and cheeks were frozen and turned black, and his left thumb had frozen inside the mitten. He concluded that he would escape with the loss of the first joint.

Then it was, beaten into the tent by the frost, that the trail, with monstrous irony, suddenly teemed with life. Three sleds went by the first day, and two the second. Once, during each day, he fought his way out to the bank only to succumb and retreat, and each of the two times, within half-an-hour after he retreated, a sled went by.

The cold snap broke, and he was able to remain by the bank once more, and the trail died again. For a week he crouched and watched, and never life stirred along it, not a soul passed in or out. He had cut down to one biscuit night and morning, and somehow he did not seem to notice it. Sometimes he marvelled at the way life remained in him. He never would have thought it possible to endure so much.

When the trail fluttered anew with life it was life with which he could not cope. A detachment of the North-West police went by, a score of them, with many sleds and dogs; and he cowered down on the bank above, and they were unaware of the menace of death that lurked in the form of a dying man beside the trail.

His frozen thumb gave him a great deal of trouble. While watching by the bank he got into the habit of taking his mitten off and thrusting the hand inside his shirt so as to rest the thumb in the warmth of his arm-pit. A mail carrier came over the trail, and Morganson let him pass. A mail carrier was an important person, and was sure to be missed immediately.

On the first day after his last flour had gone it snowed. It was always warm when the snow fell, and he sat out the whole eight hours of daylight on the bank, without movement, terribly hungry and terribly patient, for all the world like a monstrous spider waiting for its prey. But the prey did not come, and he hobbled back to the tent through the darkness, drank quarts of spruce tea and hot water, and went to bed.

The next morning circumstance eased its grip on him. As he started to come out of the tent he saw a huge bull-moose crossing the swale some four hundred yards away. Morganson felt a surge and bound of the blood in him, and then went unaccountably weak. A nausea overpowered him, and he was compelled to sit down a moment to recover. Then he reached for his rifle and took careful aim. The first shot was a hit: he knew it; but the moose turned and broke for the wooded hillside that came down to the swale. Morganson pumped bullets wildly among the trees and brush at the fleeing animal, until it dawned upon him that he was exhausting the ammunition he needed for the sled-load of life for which he waited.

He stopped shooting, and watched. He noted the direction of the animal's flight, and, high up on the hillside in an opening among the trees, saw the trunk of a fallen pine. Continuing the moose's flight in his mind he saw that it must pass the trunk. He resolved on one more shot, and in the empty air above the trunk he aimed and steadied his wavering rifle. The animal sprang into his field of vision, with lifted fore-legs as it took the leap. He pulled the trigger. With the explosion the moose seemed to somersault in the air. It crashed down to earth in the snow beyond and flurried the snow into dust.

Morganson dashed up the hillside—at least he started to dash up. The next he knew he was coming out of a faint and dragging himself to his feet. He went up more slowly, pausing from time to time to breathe and to steady his reeling senses. At last he crawled over the trunk. The moose lay before him. He sat down heavily upon the carcass and laughed. He buried his face in his mittened hands and laughed some more.

He shook the hysteria from him. He drew his hunting knife and worked as rapidly as his injured thumb and weakness would permit him. He did not stop to skin the moose, but quartered it with its hide on. It was a Klondike of meat.

When he had finished he selected a piece of meat weighing a hundred pounds, and started to drag it down to the tent. But the snow was soft, and it was too much for him. He exchanged it for a twenty-pound piece, and, with many pauses to rest, succeeded in getting it to the tent. He fried some of the meat, but ate sparingly. Then, and automatically, he went out to his crouching place on the bank. There were sled-tracks in the fresh snow on the trail. The sled-load of life had passed by while he had been cutting up the moose.

But he did not mind. He was glad that the sled had not passed before the coming of the moose. The moose had changed his plans. Its meat was worth fifty cents a pound, and he was but little more than three miles from Minto. He need no longer wait for the sled-load of life. The moose was the sled-load of life. He would sell it. He would buy a couple of dogs at Minto, some food and some tobacco, and the dogs would haul him south along the trail to the sea, the sun, and civilisation.

He felt hungry. The dull, monotonous ache of hunger had now become a sharp and insistent pang. He hobbled back to the tent and fried a slice of meat. After that he smoked two whole pipefuls of dried tea leaves. Then he fried another slice of moose. He was aware of an unwonted glow of strength, and went out and chopped some firewood. He followed that up with a slice of meat. Teased on by the food, his hunger grew into an inflammation. It became imperative every little while to fry a slice of meat. He tried smaller slices and found himself frying oftener.

In the middle of the day he thought of the wild animals that might eat his meat, and he climbed the hill, carrying along his axe, the haul rope, and a sled lashing. In his weak state the making of the cache and storing of the meat was an all-afternoon task. He cut young saplings, trimmed them, and tied them together into a tall scaffold. It was not so strong a cache as he would have desired to make, but he had done his best. To hoist the meat to the top was heart-breaking. The larger pieces defied him until he passed the rope over a limb above, and, with one end fast to a piece of meat, put all his weight on the other end.

Once in the tent, he proceeded to indulge in a prolonged and solitary orgy. He did not need friends. His stomach and he were company. Slice after slice and many slices of meat he fried and ate. He ate pounds of the meat. He brewed real tea, and brewed it strong. He brewed the last he had. It did not matter. On the morrow he would be buying tea in Minto. When it seemed he could eat no more, he smoked. He smoked all his stock of dried tea leaves. What of it? On the morrow he would be smoking tobacco. He knocked out his pipe, fried a final slice, and went to bed. He had eaten so much he seemed bursting, yet he got out of his blankets and had just one more mouthful of meat.

In the morning he awoke as from the sleep of death. In his ears were strange sounds. He did not know where he was, and looked about him stupidly until he caught sight of the frying-pan with the last piece of meat in it, partly eaten. Then he remembered all, and with a quick start turned his attention to the strange sounds. He sprang from the blankets with an oath. His scurvy-ravaged legs gave under him and he winced with the pain. He proceeded more slowly to put on his moccasins and leave the tent.

From the cache up the hillside arose a confused noise of snapping and snarling, punctuated by occasional short, sharp yelps. He increased his speed at much expense of pain, and cried loudly and threateningly. He saw the wolves hurrying away through the snow and underbrush, many of them, and he saw the scaffold down on the ground. The animals were heavy with the meat they had eaten, and they were content to slink away and leave the wreckage.

The way of the disaster was clear to him. The wolves had scented his cache. One of them had leapt from the trunk of the fallen tree to the top of the cache. He could see marks of the brute's paws in the snow that covered the trunk. He had not dreamt a wolf could leap so far. A second had followed the first, and a third and fourth, until the flimsy scaffold had gone down under their weight and movement.

His eyes were hard and savage for a moment as he contemplated the extent of the calamity; then the old look of patience returned into them, and he began to gather together the bones well picked and gnawed. There was marrow in them, he knew; and also, here and there, as he sifted the snow, he found scraps of meat that had escaped the maws of the brutes made careless by plenty.

He spent the rest of the morning dragging the wreckage of the moose down the hillside. In addition, he had at least ten pounds left of the chunk of meat he had dragged down the previous day.

"I'm good for weeks yet," was his comment as he surveyed the heap.

He had learnt how to starve and live. He cleaned his rifle and counted the cartridges that remained to him. There were seven. He loaded the weapon and hobbled out to his crouching-place on the bank. All day he watched the dead trail. He watched all the week, but no life passed over it.

Thanks to the meat he felt stronger, though his scurvy was worse and more painful. He now lived upon soup, drinking endless gallons of the thin product of the boiling of the moose bones. The soup grew thinner and thinner as he cracked the bones and boiled them over and over; but the hot water with the essence of the meat in it was good for him, and he was more vigorous than he had been previous to the shooting of the moose.

It was in the next week that a new factor entered into Morganson's life. He wanted to know the date. It became an obsession. He pondered and calculated, but his conclusions were rarely twice the same. The first thing in the morning and the last thing at night, and all day as well, watching by the trail, he worried about it. He awoke at night and lay awake for hours over the problem. To have known the date would have been of no value to him; but his curiosity grew until it equalled his hunger and his desire to live. Finally it mastered him, and he resolved to go to Minto and find out.

It was dark when he arrived at Minto, but this served him. No one saw him arrive. Besides, he knew he would have moonlight by which to return. He climbed the bank and pushed open the saloon door. The light dazzled him. The source of it was several candles, but he had been living for long in an unlighted tent. As his eyes adjusted themselves, he saw three men sitting around the stove. They were trail-travellers—he knew it at once; and since they had not passed in, they were evidently bound out. They would go by his tent next morning.

The barkeeper emitted a long and marvelling whistle.

"I thought you was dead," he said.

"Why?" Morganson asked in a faltering voice.

He had become unused to talking, and he was not acquainted with the sound of his own voice. It seemed hoarse and strange.

"You've been dead for more'n two months, now," the barkeeper explained. "You left here going south, and you never arrived at Selkirk. Where have you been?"

"Chopping wood for the steamboat company," Morganson lied unsteadily.

He was still trying to become acquainted with his own voice. He hobbled across the floor and leant against the bar. He knew he must lie consistently; and while he maintained an appearance of careless indifference, his heart was beating and pounding furiously and irregularly, and he could not help looking hungrily at the three men by the stove. They were the possessors of life—his life.

"But where in hell you been keeping yourself all this time?" the barkeeper demanded.

"I located across the river," he answered. "I've got a mighty big stack of wood chopped."

The barkeeper nodded. His face beamed with understanding.

"I heard sounds of chopping several times," he said. "So that was you, eh? Have a drink?"

Morganson clutched the bar tightly. A drink! He could have thrown his arms around the man's legs and kissed his feet. He tried vainly to utter his acceptance; but the barkeeper had not waited and was already passing out the bottle.

"But what did you do for grub?" the latter asked. "You don't look as if you could chop wood to keep yourself warm. You look terribly bad, friend."

Morganson yearned towards the delayed bottle and gulped dryly.

"I did the chopping before the scurvy got bad," he said. "Then I got a moose right at the start. I've been living high all right. It's the scurvy that's run me down."

He filled the glass, and added, "But the spruce tea's knocking it, I think."

"Have another," the barkeeper said.

The action of the two glasses of whisky on Morganson's empty stomach and weak condition was rapid. The next he knew he was sitting by the stove on a box, and it seemed as though ages had passed. A tall, broad-shouldered, black-whiskered man was paying for drinks. Morganson's swimming eyes saw him drawing a greenback from a fat roll, and Morganson's swimming eyes cleared on the instant. They were hundred-dollar bills. It was life! His life! He felt an almost irresistible impulse to snatch the money and dash madly out into the night.

The black-whiskered man and one of his companions arose.

"Come on, Oleson," the former said to the third one of the party, a fair-haired, ruddy-faced giant.

Oleson came to his feet, yawning and stretching.

"What are you going to bed so soon for?" the barkeeper asked plaintively. "It's early yet."

"Got to make Selkirk to-morrow," said he of the black whiskers.

"On Christmas Day!" the barkeeper cried.

"The better the day the better the deed," the other laughed.

As the three men passed out of the door it came dimly to Morganson that it was Christmas Eve. That was the date. That was what he had come to Minto for. But it was overshadowed now by the three men themselves, and the fat roll of hundred-dollar bills.

The door slammed.

"That's Jack Thompson," the barkeeper said. "Made two millions on Bonanza and Sulphur, and got more coming. I'm going to bed. Have another drink first."

Morganson hesitated.

"A Christmas drink," the other urged. "It's all right. I'll get it back when you sell your wood."

Morganson mastered his drunkenness long enough to swallow the whisky, say good night, and get out on the trail. It was moonlight, and he hobbled along through the bright, silvery quiet, with a vision of life before him that took the form of a roll of hundred-dollar bills.

He awoke. It was dark, and he was in his blankets. He had gone to bed in his moccasins and mittens, with the flaps of his cap pulled down over his ears. He got up as quickly as his crippled condition would permit, and built the fire and boiled some water. As he put the spruce-twigs into the teapot he noted the first glimmer of the pale morning light. He caught up his rifle and hobbled in a panic out to the bank. As he crouched and waited, it came to him that he had forgotten to drink his spruce tea. The only other thought in his mind was the possibility of John Thompson changing his mind and not travelling Christmas Day.

Dawn broke and merged into day. It was cold and clear. Sixty below zero was Morganson's estimate of the frost. Not a breath stirred the chill Arctic quiet. He sat up suddenly, his muscular tensity increasing the hurt of the scurvy. He had heard the far sound of a man's voice and the faint whining of dogs. He began beating his hands back and forth against his sides. It was a serious matter to bare the trigger hand to sixty degrees below zero, and against that time he needed to develop all the warmth of which his flesh was capable.

They came into view around the outjutting clump of trees. To the fore was the third man whose name he had not learnt. Then came eight dogs drawing the sled. At the front of the sled, guiding it by the gee-pole, walked John Thompson. The rear was brought up by Oleson, the Swede. He was certainly a fine man, Morganson thought, as he looked at the bulk of him in his squirrel-skin *parka*. The men and dogs were silhouetted sharply against the white of the landscape. They had the seeming of two dimension, cardboard figures that worked mechanically.

Morganson rested his cocked rifle in the notch in the tree. He became abruptly aware that his fingers were cold, and discovered that his right hand was bare. He did not know that he had taken off the mitten. He slipped it on again hastily. The men and dogs drew closer, and he could see their breaths spouting into visibility in the cold air. When the first man was fifty yards away, Morganson slipped the mitten from his right hand. He placed the first finger on the trigger and aimed low. When he fired the first man whirled half around and went down on the trail.

In the instant of surprise, Morganson pulled the trigger on

John Thompson—too low, for the latter staggered and sat down suddenly on the sled. Morganson raised his aim and fired again. John Thompson sank down backward along the top of the loaded sled.

Morganson turned his attention to Oleson. At the same time that he noted the latter running away towards Minto he noted that the dogs, coming to where the first man's body blocked the trail, had halted. Morganson fired at the fleeing man and missed, and Oleson swerved. He continued to swerve back and forth, while Morganson fired twice in rapid succession and missed both shots. Morganson stopped himself just as he was pulling the trigger again. He had fired six shots. Only one more cartridge remained, and it was in the chamber. It was imperative that he should not miss his last shot.

He held his fire and desperately studied Oleson's flight. The giant was grotesquely curving and twisting and running at top speed along the trail, the tail of his *parka* flapping smartly behind. Morganson trained his rifle on the man and with a swaying action followed his erratic flight. Morganson's finger was getting numb. He could scarcely feel the trigger. "God help me," he breathed a prayer aloud, and pulled the trigger. The running man pitched forward on his face, rebounded from the hard trail, and slid along, rolling over and over. He threshed for a moment with his arms and then lay quiet.

Morganson dropped his rifle (worthless now that the last cartridge was gone) and slid down the bank through the soft snow. Now that he had sprung the trap, concealment of his lurking-place was no longer necessary. He hobbled along the trail to the sled, his fingers making involuntary gripping and clutching movements inside the mittens.

The snarling of the dogs halted him. The leader, a heavy dog, half Newfoundland and half Hudson Bay, stood over the body of the man that lay on the trail, and menaced Morganson with bristling hair and bared fangs. The other seven dogs of the team were likewise bristling and snarling. Morganson approached tentatively, and the team surged towards him. He stopped again and talked to the animals, threatening and cajoling by turns. He noticed the face of the man under the leader's feet, and was surprised at how quickly it had turned white with the ebb of life and the entrance of the frost. John Thompson lay back along the top of the loaded sled, his head sunk in a space between two sacks and his chin tilted upwards, so that all Morganson could see was the black beard pointing skyward.

Finding it impossible to face the dogs Morganson stepped off the trail into the deep snow and floundered in a wide circle to the rear of the sled. Under the initiative of the leader, the team swung around in its tangled harness. Because of his crippled condition, Morganson could move only slowly. He saw the animals circling around on him and tried to retreat. He almost made it, but the big leader, with a savage lunge, sank its teeth into the calf of his leg. The flesh was slashed and torn, but Morganson managed to drag himself clear.

He cursed the brutes fiercely, but could not cow them. They replied with neck-bristling and snarling, and with quick lunges against their breastbands. He remembered Oleson, and turned his back upon them and went along the trail. He scarcely took notice of his lacerated leg. It was bleeding freely; the main artery had been torn, but he did not know it.

Especially remarkable to Morganson was the extreme pallor of the Swede, who the preceding night had been so ruddy-faced. Now his face was like white marble. What with his fair hair and lashes he looked like a carved statue rather than something that had been a man a few minutes before. Morganson pulled off his mittens and searched the body. There was no money-belt around the waist next to the skin, nor did he find a gold-sack. In a breast pocket he lit on a small wallet. With fingers that swiftly went numb with the frost, he hurried through the contents of the wallet. There were letters with foreign stamps and postmarks on them, and several receipts and memorandum accounts, and a letter of credit for eight hundred dollars. That was all. There was no money.

He made a movement to start back toward the sled, but found his foot rooted to the trail. He glanced down and saw that he stood in a fresh deposit of frozen red. There was red ice on his torn pants leg and on the moccasin beneath. With a quick effort he broke the frozen clutch of his blood and hobbled along the trail to the sled. The big leader that had bitten him began snarling and lunging, and was followed in this conduct by the whole team.

Morganson wept weakly for a space, and weakly swayed from one side to the other. Then he brushed away the frozen tears that gemmed his lashes. It was a joke. Malicious chance was having its laugh at him. Even John Thompson, with his heaven-aspiring whiskers, was laughing at him.

He prowled around the sled demented, at times weeping and pleading with the brutes for his life there on the sled, at other times raging impotently against them. Then calmness came upon him. He had been making a fool of himself. All he had to do was to go to the tent, get the axe, and return and brain the dogs. He'd show them.

In order to get to the tent he had to go wide of the sled and the savage animals. He stepped off the trail into the soft snow. Then he felt suddenly giddy and stood still. He was afraid to go on for fear he would fall down. He stood still for a long time, balancing himself on his crippled legs that were trembling violently from weakness. He looked down and saw the snow reddening at his feet. The blood flowed freely as ever. He had not thought the bite was so severe. He controlled his giddiness and stooped to examine the wound. The snow seemed rushing up to meet him, and he recoiled from it as from a blow. He had a panic fear that he might fall down, and after a struggle he managed to stand upright again. He was afraid of that snow that had rushed up to him.

Then the white glimmer turned black, and the next he knew he was awakening in the snow where he had fallen. He was no longer giddy. The cobwebs were gone. But he could not get up. There was no strength in his limbs. His body seemed lifeless. By a desperate effort he managed to roll over on his side. In this position he caught a glimpse of the sled and of John Thompson's black beard pointing skyward. Also he saw the lead dog licking the face of the man who lay on the trail. Morganson watched curiously. The dog was nervous and eager. Sometimes it uttered short, sharp yelps, as though to arouse the man, and surveyed him with ears cocked forward and wagging tail. At last it sat down, pointed its nose upward, and began to howl. Soon all the team was howling.

Now that he was down, Morganson was no longer afraid. He had a vision of himself being found dead in the snow, and for a while he wept in self-pity. But he was not afraid. The struggle had gone out of him. When he tried to open his eyes he found that the wet tears had frozen them shut. He did not try to brush the ice away. It did not matter. He had not dreamed death was so easy. He was even angry that he had struggled and suffered through so many weary weeks. He had been bullied and cheated by the fear of death. Death did not hurt. Every torment he had endured had been a torment of life. Life had defamed death. It was a cruel thing.

But his anger passed. The lies and frauds of life were of no consequence now that he was coming to his own. He became aware of drowsiness, and felt a sweet sleep stealing upon him, balmy with promises of easement and rest. He heard faintly the howling of the dogs, and had a fleeting thought that in the mastering of his flesh the frost no longer bit. Then the light and the thought ceased to pulse beneath the tear-gemmed eyelids, and with a tired sigh of comfort he sank into sleep.

THE END OF THE STORY

I

The table was of hand-hewn spruce boards, and the men who played whist had frequent difficulties in drawing home their tricks across the uneven surface. Though they sat in their undershirts, the sweat noduled and oozed on their faces; yet their feet, heavily moccasined and woollen-socked, tingled with the bite of the frost. Such was the difference of temperature in the small cabin between the floor level and a yard or more above it. The sheet-iron Yukon Stove roared red-hot, yet, eight feet away, on the meat-shelf, placed low and beside the door, lay chunks of solidly frozen moose and bacon. The door, a third of the way up from the bottom, was a thick rime. In the chinking between the logs at the back of the bunks the frost showed white and glistening. A window of oiled paper furnished light. The lower portion of the paper, on the inside, was coated an inch deep with the frozen moisture of the men's breath.

They played a momentous rubber of whist, for the pair that lost was to dig a fishing hole through the seven feet of ice and snow that covered the Yukon.

"It's mighty unusual, a cold snap like this in March," remarked the man who shuffled. "What would you call it, Bob?"

"Oh, fifty-five or sixty below—all of that. What do you make it, Doc?"

Doc turned his head and glanced at the lower part of the door with a measuring eye.

"Not a bit worse than fifty. If anything, slightly under—say forty-nine. See the ice on the door. It's just about the fifty mark, but you'll notice the upper edge is ragged. The time she went seventy the ice climbed a full four inches higher." He picked up his hand, and without ceasing from sorting called "Come in," to a knock on the door.

The man who entered was a big, broad-shouldered Swede, though his nationality was not discernible until he had removed his ear-flapped cap and thawed away the ice which had formed on beard and moustache and which served to mask his face. While engaged in this, the men at the table played out the hand.

"I hear one doctor faller stop this camp," the Swede said inquiringly, looking anxiously from face to face, his own face haggard and drawn from severe and long endured pain. "I come long way. North fork of the Whyo."

"I'm the doctor. What's the matter?"

In response, the man held up his left hand, the second finger of which was monstrously swollen. At the same time he began a rambling, disjointed history of the coming and growth of his affliction.

"Let me look at it," the doctor broke in impatiently. "Lay it on the table. There, like that."

Tenderly, as if it were a great boil, the man obeyed.

"Humph," the doctor grumbled. "A weeping sinew. And travelled a hundred miles to have it fixed. I'll fix it in a jiffy. You watch me, and next time you can do it yourself."

Without warning, squarely and at right angles, and savagely, the doctor brought the edge of his hand down on the swollen crooked finger. The man yelled with consternation and agony. It was more like the cry of a wild beast, and his face was a wild beast's as he was about to spring on the man who had perpetrated the joke.

"That's all right," the doctor placated sharply and authoritatively. "How do you feel? Better, eh? Of course. Next time you can do it yourself—Go on and deal, Strothers. I think we've got you."

Slow and ox-like, on the face of the Swede dawned relief and comprehension. The pang over, the finger felt better. The pain was gone. He examined the finger curiously, with wondering eyes, slowly crooking it back and forth. He reached into his pocket and pulled out a gold-sack.

"How much?"

The doctor shook his head impatiently. "Nothing. I'm not practising—Your play, Bob."

The Swede moved heavily on his feet, re-examined the finger, then turned an admiring gaze on the doctor.

"You are good man. What your name?"

"Linday, Doctor Linday," Strothers answered, as if solicitous to save his opponent from further irritation.

"The day's half done," Linday said to the Swede, at the end of the hand, while he shuffled. "Better rest over to-night. It's too cold for travelling. There's a spare bunk."

He was a slender brunette of a man, lean-cheeked, thin-lipped, and strong. The smooth-shaven face was a healthy sallow. All his movements were quick and precise. He did not fumble his cards. The eyes were black, direct, and piercing, with the trick of seeming to look beneath the surfaces of things. His hands, slender, fine and nervous, appeared made for delicate work, and to the most casual eye they conveyed an impression of strength.

"Our game," he announced, drawing in the last trick. "Now for the rub and who digs the fishing hole."

A knock at the door brought a quick exclamation from him.

"Seems we just can't finish this rubber," he complained, as the door opened. "What's the matter with *you*?"—this last to the stranger who entered.

The newcomer vainly strove to move his icebound jaws and jowls. That he had been on trail for long hours and days was patent. The skin across the cheekbones was black with repeated frost-bite. From nose to chin was a mass of solid ice perforated by the hole through which he breathed. Through this he had also spat tobacco juice, which had frozen, as it trickled, into an amber-coloured icicle, pointed like a Van Dyke beard.

He shook his head dumbly, grinned with his eyes, and drew near to the stove to thaw his mouth to speech. He assisted the process with his fingers, clawing off fragments of melting ice which rattled and sizzled on the stove.

"Nothing the matter with me," he finally announced. "But if they's a doctor in the outfit he's sure needed. They's a man up the Little Peco that's had a ruction with a panther, an' the way he's clawed is something scand'lous."

"How far up?" Doctor Linday demanded.

"A matter of a hundred miles."

"How long since?"

"I've ben three days comin' down."

"Bad?"

"Shoulder dislocated. Some ribs broke for sure. Right arm broke. An' clawed clean to the bone most all over but the face. We sewed up two or three bad places temporary, and tied arteries with twine."

"That settles it," Linday sneered. "Where were they?"

"Stomach."

"He's a sight by now."

"Not on your life. Washed clean with bug-killin' dope before we stitched. Only temporary anyway. Had nothin' but linen thread, but washed that, too."

"He's as good as dead," was Linday's judgment, as he angrily fingered the cards.

"Nope. That man ain't goin' to die. He knows I've come for a doctor, an' he'll make out to live until you get there. He won't let himself die. I know him."

"Christian Science and gangrene, eh?" came the sneer. "Well, I'm not practising. Nor can I see myself travelling a hundred miles at fifty below for a dead man."

"I can see you, an' for a man a long ways from dead."

Linday shook his head. "Sorry you had your trip for nothing. Better stop over for the night."

"Nope. We'll be pullin' out in ten minutes."

"What makes you so cocksure?" Linday demanded testily.

Then it was that Tom Daw made the speech of his life.

"Because he's just goin' on livin' till you get there, if it takes you a week to make up your mind. Besides, his wife's with him, not sheddin' a tear, or nothin', an' she's helpin' him live till you come. They think a almighty heap of each other, an' she's got a will like hisn. If he weakened, she'd just put her immortal soul into hisn an' make him live. Though he ain't weakenin' none, you can stack on that. I'll stack on it. I'll lay you three to one, in ounces, he's alive when you get there. I got a team of dawgs down the bank. You ought to allow to start in ten minutes, an' we ought to make it back in less'n three days because the trail's broke. I'm goin' down to the dawgs now, an' I'll look for you in ten minutes."

Tom Daw pulled down his earflaps, drew on his mittens, and passed out.

"Damn him!" Linday cried, glaring vindictively at the closed door.

II

That night, long after dark, with twenty-five miles behind them, Linday and Tom Daw went into camp. It was a simple but adequate affair: a fire built in the snow; alongside, their sleeping-furs spread in a single bed on a mat of spruce boughs; behind the bed an oblong of canvas stretched to refract the heat. Daw fed the dogs and chopped ice and firewood. Linday's cheeks burned with frost-bite as he squatted over the cooking. They ate heavily, smoked a pipe and talked while they dried their moccasins before the fire, and turned in to sleep the dead sleep of fatigue and health.

Morning found the unprecedented cold snap broken. Linday estimated the temperature at fifteen below and rising. Daw was worried. That day would see them in the canyon, he explained, and if the spring thaw set in the canyon would run open water. The walls of the canyon were hundreds to thousands of feet high. They could be climbed, but the going would be slow.

Camped well in the dark and forbidding gorge, over their pipe that evening they complained of the heat, and both agreed that the thermometer must be above zero—the first time in six months.

"Nobody ever heard tell of a panther this far north," Daw was saying. "Rocky called it a cougar. But I shot a-many of 'em down in Curry County, Oregon, where I come from, an' we called 'em panther. Anyway, it was a bigger cat than ever I seen. It was sure a monster cat. Now how'd it ever stray to such out of the way huntin' range?—that's the question."

Linday made no comment. He was nodding. Propped on sticks, his moccasins steamed unheeded and unturned. The dogs, curled in furry balls, slept in the snow. The crackle of an ember accentuated the profound of silence that reigned. He awoke with a start and gazed at Daw, who nodded and returned the gaze. Both listened. From far off came a vague disturbance that increased to a vast and sombre roaring. As it neared, ever-increasing, riding the mountain tops as well as the canyon depths, bowing the forest before it, bending the meagre, crevice-rooted pines on the walls of the gorge, they knew it for what it was. A wind, strong and warm, a balmy gale, drove past them, flinging a rocket-shower of sparks from the fire. The dogs, aroused, sat on their haunches, bleak noses pointed upward, and raised the long wolf howl.

"It's the Chinook," Daw said.

"It means the river trail, I suppose?"

"Sure thing. And ten miles of it is easier than one over the tops." Daw surveyed Linday for a long, considering minute. "We've just had fifteen hours of trail," he shouted above the wind, tentatively, and again waited. "Doc," he said finally, "are you game?"

For answer, Linday knocked out his pipe and began to pull on his damp moccasins. Between them, and in few minutes, bending to the force of the wind, the dogs were harnessed, camp broken, and the cooking outfit and unused sleeping furs lashed on the sled. Then, through the darkness, for a night of travel, they churned out on the trail Daw had broken nearly a week before. And all through the night the Chinook roared and they urged the weary dogs and spurred their own jaded muscles. Twelve hours of it they made, and stopped for breakfast after twenty-seven hours on trail.

"An hour's sleep," said Daw, when they had wolfed pounds of straight moose-meat fried with bacon.

Two hours he let his companion sleep, afraid himself to close his eyes. He occupied himself with making marks upon the soft-surfaced, shrinking snow. Visibly it shrank. In two hours the snow level sank three inches. From every side, faintly heard and near, under the voice of the spring wind, came the trickling of hidden waters. The Little Peco, strengthened by the multitudinous streamlets, rose against the manacles of winter, riving the ice with crashings and snappings.

Daw touched Linday on the shoulder; touched him again; shook, and shook violently.

"Doc," he murmured admiringly. "You can sure go some."

The weary black eyes, under heavy lids, acknowledged the compliment.

"But that ain't the question. Rocky is clawed something scand'lous. As I said before, I helped sew up his in'ards. Doc...." He shook the man, whose eyes had again closed. "I say, Doc! The question is: can you go some more?—hear me? I say, can you go some more?"

The weary dogs snapped and whimpered when kicked from their sleep. The going was slow, not more than two miles an hour, and the animals took every opportunity to lie down in the wet snow.

"Twenty miles of it, and we'll be through the gorge," Daw encouraged. 'After that the ice can go to blazes, for we can take to the bank, and it's only ten more miles to camp. Why, Doc, we're almost there. And when you get Rocky fixed up, you can come down in a canoe in one day."

But the ice grew more uneasy under them, breaking loose from the shore-line and rising steadily inch by inch. In places where it still held to the shore, the water overran and they waded and slushed across. The Little Peco growled and muttered. Cracks and fissures were forming everywhere as they battled on for the miles that each one of which meant ten along the tops.

"Get on the sled, Doc, an' take a snooze," Daw invited.

The glare from the black eyes prevented him from repeating the suggestion.

As early as midday they received definite warning of the beginning of the end. Cakes of ice, borne downward in the rapid current, began to thunder beneath the ice on which they stood. The dogs whimpered anxiously and yearned for the bank.

"That means open water above," Daw explained. "Pretty soon she'll jam somewheres, an' the river'll raise a hundred feet in a hundred minutes. It's us for the tops if we can find a way to climb out. Come on! Hit her up I! An' just to think, the Yukon'll stick solid for weeks."

Unusually narrow at this point, the great walls of the canyon were too precipitous to scale. Daw and Linday had to keep on; and they kept on till the disaster happened. With a loud explosion, the ice broke asunder midway under the team. The two animals in the middle of the string went into the fissure, and the grip of the current on their bodies dragged the lead-dog backward and in. Swept downstream under the ice, these three bodies began to drag to the edge the two whining dogs that remained. The men held back frantically on the sled, but were slowly drawn along with it. It was all over in the space of seconds. Daw slashed the wheel-dog's traces with his sheath-knife, and the animal whipped over the ice-edge and was gone. The ice on which they stood, broke into a large and pivoting cake that ground and splintered against the shore ice and rocks. Between them they got the sled ashore and up into a crevice in time to see the ice-cake up-edge, sink, and down-shelve from view.

Meat and sleeping furs were made into packs, and the sled was abandoned. Linday resented Daw's taking the heavier pack, but Daw had his will.

"You got to work as soon as you get there. Come on."

It was one in the afternoon when they started to climb. At eight that evening they cleared the rim and for half an hour lay where they had fallen. Then came the fire, a pot of coffee, and an enormous feed of moosemeat. But first Linday hefted the two packs, and found his own lighter by half.

"You're an iron man, Daw," he admired.

"Who?" Me? Oh, pshaw! You ought to see Rocky. He's made out of platinum, an' armour plate, an' pure gold, an' all strong things. I'm mountaineer, but he plumb beats me out. Down in Curry County I used to 'most kill the boys when we run bear. So when I hooks up with Rocky on our first hunt I had a mean idea to show 'm a few. I let out the links good an' generous, 'most nigh keepin' up with the dawgs, an' along comes Rocky a-treadin' on my heels. I knowed he couldn't last that way, and I just laid down an' did my dangdest. An' there he was, at the end of another hour, a-treadin' steady an' regular on my heels. I was some huffed. 'Mebbe you'd like to come to the front an' show me how to travel,' I says. 'Sure,' says he. An' he done it! I stayed with 'm, but let me tell you I was plumb tuckered by the time the bear tree'd.

"They ain't no stoppin' that man. He ain't afraid of nothin'. Last fall, before the freeze-up, him an' me was headin' for camp about twilight. I was clean shot out—ptarmigan—an' he had one cartridge left. An' the dawgs tree'd a she grizzly. Small one. Only weighed about three hundred, but you know what grizzlies is. 'Don't do it,' says I, when he ups with his rifle. 'You only got that one shot, an' it's too dark to see the sights.'"

"'Climb a tree,' says he. I didn't climb no tree, but when that bear come down a-cussin' among the dawgs, an' only creased, I want to tell you I was sure hankerin' for a tree. It was some ruction. Then things come on real bad. The bear slid down a hollow against a big log. Downside, that log was four feet up an' down. Dawgs couldn't get at bear that way. Upside was steep gravel, an' the dawgs'd just naturally slide down into the bear. They was no jumpin' back, an' the bear was a-manglin' 'em fast as they come. All underbrush, gettin' pretty dark, no cartridges, nothin'."

"What's Rocky up an' do? He goes downside of log, reaches over with his knife, an' begins slashin'. But he can only reach bear's rump, an' dawgs bein' ruined fast, one-two-three time. Rocky gets desperate. He don't like to lose his dawgs. He jumps on top log, grabs bear by the slack of the rump, an' heaves over back'ard right over top of that log. Down they go, kit an' kaboodle, twenty feet, bear, dawgs, an' Rocky, slidin', cussin', an' scratchin', ker-plump into ten feet of water in the bed of stream. They all swum out different ways. Nope, he didn't get the bear, but he saved the dawgs. That's Rocky. They's no stoppin' him when his mind's set."

It was at the next camp that Linday heard how Rocky had come to be injured.

"I'd ben up the draw, about a mile from the cabin, lookin' for a piece of birch likely enough for an axe-handle. Comin' back I heard the darndest goings-on where we had a bear trap set. Some trapper had left the trap in an old cache an' Rocky'd fixed it up. But the goings-on. It was Rocky an' his brother Harry. First I'd hear one yell and laugh, an' then the other, like it was some game. An' what do you think the fool game was? I've saw some pretty nervy cusses down in Curry County, but they beat all. They'd got a whoppin' big panther in the trap an' was takin' turns rappin' it on the nose with a light stick. But that wa'n't the point. I just come out of the brush in time to see Harry rap it. Then he chops six inches off the stick an' passes it to Rocky. You see, that stick was growin' shorter all the time. It ain't as easy as you think. The panther'd slack back an' hunch down an' spit, an' it was mighty lively in duckin' the stick. An' you never knowed when it'd jump. It was caught by the hind leg, which was curious, too, an' it had some slack I'm tellin' you.

"It was just a game of dare they was playin', an' the stick gettin' shorter an' shorter an' the panther madder 'n madder. Bimeby they wa'n't no stick left—only a nubbin, about four inches long, an' it was Rocky's turn. 'Better quit now,' says Harry. 'What for?' says Rocky. 'Because if you rap him again they won't be no stick left for me,' Harry answers. 'Then you'll quit an' I win,' says Rocky with a laugh, an' goes to it.

"An' I don't want to see anything like it again. That cat'd bunched back an' down till it had all of six feet slack in its body. An' Rocky's stick four inches long. The cat got him. You couldn't see one from t'other. No chance to shoot. It was Harry, in the end, that got his knife into the panther's jugular."

"If I'd known how he got it I'd never have come," was Linday's comment.

Daw nodded concurrence.

"That's what she said. She told me sure not to whisper how it happened."

"Is he crazy?' Linday demanded in his wrath.

"They're all crazy. Him an' his brother are all the time devilin' each other to tom-fool things. I seen them swim the riffle last fall, bad water an' mush-ice runnin'—on a dare. They ain't nothin' they won't tackle. An' she's 'most as bad. Not afraid some herself. She'll do anything Rocky'll let her. But he's almighty careful with her. Treats her like a queen. No camp-work or such for her. That's why another man an' me are hired on good wages. They've got slathers of money an' they're sure dippy on each other. 'Looks like good huntin',' says Rocky, when they struck that section last fall. 'Let's make a camp then,' says Harry. An' me all the time thinkin' they was lookin' for gold. Ain't ben a prospect pan washed the whole winter."

Linday's anger mounted. "I haven't any patience with fools. For two cents I'd turn back."

"No you wouldn't," Daw assured him confidently. "They ain't enough grub to turn back, an' we'll be there to-morrow. Just got to cross that last divide an' drop down to the cabin. An' they's a better reason. You're too far from home, an' I just naturally wouldn't let you turn back."

Exhausted as Linday was, the flash in his black eyes warned Daw that he had overreached himself. His hand went out.

"My mistake, Doc. Forget it. I reckon I'm gettin' some cranky what of losin' them dawgs."

III

Not one day, but three days later, the two men, after being snowed in on the summit by a spring blizzard, staggered up to a cabin that stood in a fat bottom beside the roaring Little Peco. Coming in from the bright sunshine to the dark cabin, Linday observed little of its occupants. He was no more than aware of two men and a woman. But he was not interested in them. He went directly to the bunk where lay the injured man. The latter was lying on his back, with eyes closed, and Linday noted the slender stencilling of the brows and the kinky silkiness of the brown hair. Thin and wan, the face seemed too small for the muscular neck, yet the delicate features, despite their waste, were firmly moulded.

"What dressings have you been using?" Linday asked of the woman.

"Corrosive, sublimate, regular solution," came the answer.

He glanced quickly at her, shot an even quicker glance at the face of the injured man, and stood erect. She breathed sharply, abruptly biting off the respiration with an effort of will. Linday turned to the men.

"You clear out—chop wood or something. Clear out."

One of them demurred.

"This is a serious case," Linday went on. "I want to talk to his wife."

"I'm his brother," said the other.

To him the woman looked, praying him with her eyes. He nodded reluctantly and turned toward the door.

"Me, too?" Daw queried from the bench where he had flung

himself down.

"You, too."

Linday busied himself with a superficial examination of the patient while the cabin was emptying.

"So?" he said. "So that's your Rex Strang."

She dropped her eyes to the man in the bunk as if to reassure herself of his identity, and then in silence returned Linday's gaze.

"Why don't you speak?"

She shrugged her shoulders. "What is the use? You know it is Rex Strang."

"Thank you. Though I might remind you that it is the first time I have ever seen him. Sit down." He waved her to a stool, himself taking the bench. "I'm really about all in, you know. There's no turnpike from the Yukon here."

He drew a penknife and began extracting a thorn from his thumb.

"What are you going to do?" she asked, after a minute's wait.

"Eat and rest up before I start back."

"What are you going to do about...." She inclined her head toward the unconscious man.

"Nothing."

She went over to the bunk and rested her fingers lightly on the tight-curled hair.

"You mean you will kill him," she said slowly. "Kill him by

doing nothing, for you can save him if you will."

"Take it that way." He considered a moment, and stated his thought with a harsh little laugh. "From time immemorial in this weary old world it has been a not uncommon custom so to dispose of wife-stealers."

"You are unfair, Grant," she answered gently. "You forget that I was willing and that I desired. I was a free agent. Rex never stole me. It was you who lost me. I went with him, willing and eager, with song on my lips. As well accuse me of stealing him. We went together."

"A good way of looking at it," Linday conceded. "I see you are as keen a thinker as ever, Madge. That must have bothered him."

"A keen thinker can be a good lover—"

"And not so foolish," he broke in.

"Then you admit the wisdom of my course?"

He threw up his hands. "That's the devil of it, talking with clever women. A man always forgets and traps himself. I wouldn't wonder if you won him with a syllogism."

Her reply was the hint of a smile in her straight-looking blue eyes and a seeming emanation of sex pride from all the physical being of her.

"No, I take that back, Madge. If you'd been a numbskull you'd have won him, or any one else, on your looks, and form, and carriage. I ought to know. I've been through that particular mill, and, the devil take me, I'm not through it yet."

His speech was quick and nervous and irritable, as it always was, and, as she knew, it was always candid. She took her cue from his last remark.

"Do you remember Lake Geneva?"

"I ought to. I was rather absurdly happy."

She nodded, and her eyes were luminous. "There is such a thing as old sake. Won't you, Grant, please, just remember back ... a little ... oh, so little ... of what we were to each other ... then?"

"Now you're taking advantage," he smiled, and returned to the attack on his thumb. He drew the thorn out, inspected it critically, then concluded. "No, thank you. I'm not playing the Good Samaritan."

"Yet you made this hard journey for an unknown man," she urged.

His impatience was sharply manifest. "Do you fancy I'd have moved a step had I known he was my wife's lover?"

"But you are here ... now. And there he lies. What are you going to do?"

"Nothing. Why should I? I am not at the man's service. He pilfered me."

She was about to speak, when a knock came on the door.

"Get out!" he shouted.

"If you want any assistance—"

"Get out! Get a bucket of water! Set it down outside!"

"You are going to...?" she began tremulously.

"Wash up."

She recoiled from the brutality, and her lips tightened.

"Listen, Grant," she said steadily. "I shall tell his brother. I know the Strang breed. If you can forget old sake, so can I. If you don't do something, he'll kill you. Why, even Tom Daw would if I asked."

"You should know me better than to threaten," he reproved gravely, then added, with a sneer: "Besides, I don't see how killing me will help your Rex Strang."

She gave a low gasp, closed her lips tightly, and watched his quick eyes take note of the trembling that had beset her.

"It's not hysteria, Grant," she cried hastily and anxiously, with clicking teeth. "You never saw me with hysteria. I've never had it. I don't know what it is, but I'll control it. I am merely beside myself. It's partly anger—with you. And it's apprehension and fear. I don't want to lose him. I do love him, Grant. He is my king, my lover. And I have sat here beside him so many dreadful days now. Oh, Grant, please, please."

"Just nerves," he commented drily. "Stay with it. You can best it. If you were a man I'd say take a smoke."

She went unsteadily back to the stool, where she watched him and fought for control. From the rough fireplace came the singing of a cricket. Outside two wolf-dogs bickered. The injured man's chest rose and fell perceptibly under the fur robes. She saw a smile, not altogether pleasant, form on Linday's lips.

"How much do you love him?" he asked.

Her breast filled and rose, and her eyes shone with a light unashamed and proud. He nodded in token that he was answered.

"Do you mind if I take a little time?" He stopped, casting about for the way to begin. "I remember reading a story— Herbert Shaw wrote it, I think. I want to tell you about it.

There was a woman, young and beautiful; a man magnificent, a lover of beauty and a wanderer. I don't know how much like your Rex Strang he was, but I fancy a sort of resemblance. Well, this man was a painter, a bohemian, a vagabond. He kissed—oh, several times and for several weeks—and rode away. She possessed for him what I thought you possessed for me ... at Lake Geneva. In ten years she wept the beauty out of her face. Some women turn yellow, you know, when grief upsets their natural juices.

"Now it happened that the man went blind, and ten years afterward, led as a child by the hand, he stumbled back to her. There was nothing left. He could no longer paint. And she was very happy, and glad he could not see her face. Remember, he worshipped beauty. And he continued to hold her in his arms and believe in her beauty. The memory of it was vivid in him. He never ceased to talk about it, and to lament that he could not behold it.

"One day he told her of five great pictures he wished to paint. If only his sight could be restored to paint them, he could write *finis* and be content. And then, no matter how, there came into her hands an elixir. Anointed on his eyes, the sight would surely and fully return."

Linday shrugged his shoulders.

"You see her struggle. With sight, he could paint his five pictures. Also, he would leave her. Beauty was his religion. It was impossible that he could abide her ruined face. Five days she struggled. Then she anointed his eyes."

Linday broke off and searched her with his eyes, the high lights focused sharply in the brilliant black.

"The question is, do you love Rex Strang as much as that?"

"And if I do?" she countered.

"Do you?"

"Yes."

"You can sacrifice? You can give him up?"

Slow and reluctant was her "Yes."

"And you will come with me?"

"Yes." This time her voice was a whisper. "When he is well—yes."

"You understand. It must be Lake Geneva over again. You will be my wife."

She seemed to shrink and droop, but her head nodded.

"Very well." He stood up briskly, went to his pack, and began unstrapping. "I shall need help. Bring his brother in. Bring them all in. Boiling water—let there be lots of it. I've brought bandages, but let me see what you have in that line.—Here, Daw, build up that fire and start boiling all the water you can.—Here you," to the other man, "get that table out and under the window there. Clean it; scrub it; scald it. Clean, man, clean, as you never cleaned a thing before. You, Mrs. Strang, will be my helper. No sheets, I suppose. Well, we'll manage somehow.—You're his brother, sir. I'll give the anaesthetic, but you must keep it going afterward. Now listen, while I instruct you. In the first place—but before that, can you take a pulse?..."

IV

Noted for his daring and success as a surgeon, through the days and weeks that followed Linday exceeded himself in daring and success. Never, because of the frightful mangling and breakage, and because of the long delay, had he encountered so terrible a case. But he had never had a healthier specimen of human wreck to work upon. Even then he would have failed, had it not been for the patient's catlike vitality and almost uncanny physical and mental grip on life.

There were days of high temperature and delirium; days of heart-sinking when Strang's pulse was barely perceptible; days when he lay conscious, eyes weary and drawn, the sweat of pain on his face. Linday was indefatigable, cruelly efficient, audacious and fortunate, daring hazard after hazard and winning. He was not content to make the man live. He devoted himself to the intricate and perilous problem of making him whole and strong again.

"He will be a cripple?" Madge queried.

"He will not merely walk and talk and be a limping caricature of his former self," Linday told her. "He shall run and leap, swim riffles, ride bears, fight panthers, and do all things to the top of his fool desire. And, I warn you, he will fascinate women just as of old. Will you like that? Are you content? Remember, you will not be with him."

"Go on, go on," she breathed. "Make him whole. Make him what he was."

More than once, whenever Strang's recuperation permitted, Linday put him under the anaesthetic and did terrible things, cutting and sewing, rewiring and connecting up the disrupted organism. Later, developed a hitch in the left arm. Strang could lift it so far, and no farther. Linday applied himself to the problem. It was a case of more wires, shrunken, twisted, disconnected. Again it was cut and switch and ease and disentangle. And all that saved Strang was his tremendous vitality and the health of his flesh.

"You will kill him," his brother complained. "Let him be. For God's sake let him be. A live and crippled man is better than a whole and dead one."

Linday flamed in wrath. "You get out! Out of this cabin with you till you can come back and say that I make him live. Pull—by God, man, you've got to pull with me with all your soul. Your brother's travelling a hairline razor-edge. Do you understand? A thought can topple him off. Now get out, and come back sweet and wholesome, convinced beyond all absoluteness that he will live and be what he was before you and he played the fool together. Get out, I say."

The brother, with clenched hands and threatening eyes, looked to Madge for counsel.

"Go, go, please," she begged. "He is right. I know he is right."

Another time, when Strang's condition seemed more promising, the brother said:

"Doc, you're a wonder, and all this time I've forgotten to ask your name."

"None of your damn business. Don't bother me. Get out."

The mangled right arm ceased from its healing, burst open again in a frightful wound.

"Necrosis," said Linday.

"That does settle it," groaned the brother.

"Shut up!" Linday snarled. "Get out! Take Daw with you. Take Bill, too. Get rabbits—alive—healthy ones. Trap them.

Trap everywhere."

"How many?" the brother asked.

"Forty of them—four thousand—forty thousand—all you can get. You'll help me, Mrs. Strang. I'm going to dig into that arm and size up the damage. Get out, you fellows. You for the rabbits."

And he dug in, swiftly, unerringly, scraping away disintegrating bone, ascertaining the extent of the active decay.

"It never would have happened," he told Madge, "if he hadn't had so many other things needing vitality first. Even he didn't have vitality enough to go around. I was watching it, but I had to wait and chance it. That piece must go. He could manage without it, but rabbit-bone will make it what it was."

From the hundreds of rabbits brought in, he weeded out, rejected, selected, tested, selected and tested again, until he made his final choice. He used the last of his chloroform and achieved the bone-graft—living bone to living bone, living man and living rabbit immovable and indissolubly bandaged and bound together, their mutual processes uniting and reconstructing a perfect arm.

And through the whole trying period, especially as Strang mended, occurred passages of talk between Linday and Madge. Nor was he kind, nor she rebellious.

"It's a nuisance," he told her. "But the law is the law, and you'll need a divorce before we can marry again. What do you say? Shall we go to Lake Geneva?"

"As you will," she said.

And he, another time: "What the deuce did you see in him anyway? I know he had money. But you and I were managing to get along with some sort of comfort. My practice was averaging around forty thousand a year then—I went over the books afterward. Palaces and steam yachts were about all that was denied you."

"Perhaps you've explained it," she answered. "Perhaps you were too interested in your practice. Maybe you forgot me."

"Humph," he sneered. "And may not your Rex be too interested in panthers and short sticks?"

He continually girded her to explain what he chose to call her infatuation for the other man.

"There is no explanation," she replied. And, finally, she retorted, "No one can explain love, I least of all. I only knew love, the divine and irrefragable fact, that is all. There was once, at Fort Vancouver, a baron of the Hudson Bay Company who chided the resident Church of England parson. The dominie had written home to England complaining that the Company folk, from the head factor down, were addicted to Indian wives. 'Why didn't you explain the extenuating circumstances?' demanded the baron. Replied the dominie: 'A cow's tail grows downward. I do not attempt to explain why the cow's tail grows downward. I merely cite the fact.'"

"Damn clever women!" cried Linday, his eyes flashing his irritation.

"What brought you, of all places, into the Klondike?" she asked once.

"Too much money. No wife to spend it. Wanted a rest. Possibly overwork. I tried Colorado, but their telegrams followed me, and some of them did themselves. I went on to Seattle. Same thing. Ransom ran his wife out to me in a special train. There was no escaping it. Operation successful. Local newspapers got wind of it. You can imagine the rest. I had to hide, so I ran away to Klondike. And—well, Tom Daw found me playing whist in a cabin down on the Yukon."

Came the day when Strang's bed was carried out of doors and into the sunshine.

"Let me tell him now," she said to Linday.

"No; wait," he answered.

Later, Strang was able to sit up on the edge of the bed, able to walk his first giddy steps, supported on either side.

"Let me tell him now," she said.

"No. I'm making a complete job of this. I want no set-backs. There's a slight hitch still in that left arm. It's a little thing, but I am going to remake him as God made him. Tomorrow I've planned to get into that arm and take out the kink. It will mean a couple of days on his back. I'm sorry there's no more chloroform. He'll just have to bite his teeth on a spike and hang on. He can do it. He's got grit for a dozen men."

Summer came on. The snow disappeared, save on the far peaks of the Rockies to the east. The days lengthened till there was no darkness, the sun dipping at midnight, due north, for a few minutes beneath the horizon. Linday never let up on Strang. He studied his walk, his body movements, stripped him again and again and for the thousandth time made him flex all his muscles. Massage was given him without end, until Linday declared that Tom Daw, Bill, and the brother were properly qualified for Turkish bath and osteopathic hospital attendants. But Linday was not yet satisfied. He put Strang through his whole repertoire of physical feats, searching him the while for hidden weaknesses. He put him on his back again for a week, opened up his leg, played a deft trick or two with the smaller veins, scraped a spot of bone no larger than a coffee grain till naught but a surface of healthy pink remained to be sewed over with the living flesh.

"Let me tell him," Madge begged.

"Not yet," was the answer. "You will tell him only when I am ready."

July passed, and August neared its end, when he ordered Strang out on trail to get a moose. Linday kept at his heels, watching him, studying him. He was slender, a cat in the strength of his muscles, and he walked as Linday had seen no man walk, effortlessly, with all his body, seeming to lift the legs with supple muscles clear to the shoulders. But it was without heaviness, so easy that it invested him with a peculiar grace, so easy that to the eye the speed was deceptive. It was the killing pace of which Tom Daw had complained. Linday toiled behind, sweating and panting; from time to time, when the ground favoured, making short runs to keep up. At the end of ten miles he called a halt and threw himself down on the moss.

"Enough!" he cried. "I can't keep up with you."

He mopped his heated face, and Strang sat down on a spruce log, smiling at the doctor, and, with the camaraderie of a pantheist, at all the landscape.

"Any twinges, or hurts, or aches, or hints of aches?" Linday demanded.

Strang shook his curly head and stretched his lithe body, living and joying in every fibre of it.

"You'll do, Strang. For a winter or two you may expect to feel the cold and damp in the old wounds. But that will pass, and perhaps you may escape it altogether."

"God, Doctor, you have performed miracles with me. I don't know how to thank you. I don't even know your name."

"Which doesn't matter. I've pulled you through, and that's the main thing."

"But it's a name men must know out in the world," Strang

persisted. "I'll wager I'd recognise it if I heard it."

"I think you would," was Linday's answer. "But it's beside the matter. I want one final test, and then I'm done with you. Over the divide at the head of this creek is a tributary of the Big Windy. Daw tells me that last year you went over, down to the middle fork, and back again, in three days. He said you nearly killed him, too. You are to wait here and camp to-night. I'll send Daw along with the camp outfit. Then it's up to you to go to the middle fork and back in the same time as last year."

V

"Now," Linday said to Madge. "You have an hour in which to pack. I'll go and get the canoe ready. Bill's bringing in the moose and won't get back till dark. We'll make my cabin to-day, and in a week we'll be in Dawson."

"I was in hope...." She broke off proudly.

"That I'd forego the fee?"

"Oh, a compact is a compact, but you needn't have been so hateful in the collecting. You have not been fair. You have sent him away for three days, and robbed me of my last words to him."

"Leave a letter."

"I shall tell him all."

"Anything less than all would be unfair to the three of us," was Linday's answer.

When he returned from the canoe, her outfit was packed, the letter written.

"Let me read it," he said, "if you don't mind."

Her hesitation was momentary, then she passed it over.

"Pretty straight," he said, when he had finished it. "Now, are you ready?"

He carried her pack down to the bank, and, kneeling, steadied the canoe with one hand while he extended the other to help her in. He watched her closely, but without a tremor she held out her hand to his and prepared to step on board.

"Wait," he said. "One moment. You remember the story I told you of the elixir. I failed to tell you the end. And when she had anointed his eyes and was about to depart, it chanced she saw in the mirror that her beauty had been restored to her. And he opened his eyes, and cried out with joy at the sight of her beauty, and folded her in his arms."

She waited, tense but controlled, for him to continue, a dawn of wonder faintly beginning to show in her face and eyes.

"You are very beautiful, Madge." He paused, then added drily, "The rest is obvious. I fancy Rex Strang's arms won't remain long empty. Good-bye."

"Grant...." she said, almost whispered, and in her voice was all the speech that needs not words for understanding.

He gave a nasty little laugh. "I just wanted to show you I wasn't such a bad sort. Coals of fire, you know."

"Grant...."

He stepped into the canoe and put out a slender, nervous hand.

"Good-bye," he said.

She folded both her own hands about his.

"Dear, strong hand," she murmured, and bent and kissed it.

He jerked it away, thrust the canoe out from the bank, dipped the paddle in the swift rush of the current, and entered the head of the riffle where the water poured glassily ere it burst into a white madness of foam.

ABOUT THE AUTHOR

 **Jack London,** probably born John Griffith Chaney (January 12, 1876 – November 22, 1916) was an American author who wrote The Call of the Wild and over fifty other books. A pioneer in the then-burgeoning world of commercial magazine fiction, he was one of the first Americans to make a huge financial success from writing.

Clarice Stasz and other biographers believe it to be likely that Jack London's biological father was astrologer William Chaney. Chaney was a professor of astrology; according to Stasz, "From the viewpoint of serious astrologers today, Chaney is a major figure who shifted the practice from quackery to a more rigorous method."

A pivotal event was his discovery in 1886 of the Oakland Public Library and a sympathetic librarian, Ina Coolbrith (who later became California's first poet laureate and an important figure in the San Francisco literary community).

In later life Jack London indulged his very wide-ranging interests with a personal library of 15,000 volumes, referring to his books as "the tools of my trade."

Choose from Thousands of 1stWorldLibrary Classics By

A. M. Barnard
Ada Leverson
Adolphus William Ward
Aesop
Agatha Christie
Alexander Aaronsohn
Alexander Kielland
Alexandre Dumas
Alfred Gatty
Alfred Ollivant
Alice Duer Miller
Alice Turner Curtis
Alice Dunbar
Allen Chapman
Alleyne Ireland
Ambrose Bierce
Amelia E. Barr
Amory H. Bradford
Andrew Lang
Andrew McFarland Davis
Andy Adams
Angela Brazil
Anna Alice Chapin
Anna Sewell
Annie Besant
Annie Hamilton Donnell
Annie Payson Call
Annie Roe Carr
Annonaymous
Anton Chekhov
Archibald Lee Fletcher
Arnold Bennett
Arthur C. Benson
Arthur Conan Doyle
Arthur M. Winfield
Arthur Ransome
Arthur Schnitzler
Arthur Train
Atticus
B.H. Baden-Powell
B. M. Bower
B. C. Chatterjee
Baroness Emmuska Orczy
Baroness Orczy
Basil King
Bayard Taylor
Ben Macomber
Bertha Muzzy Bower
Bjornstjerne Bjornson

Booth Tarkington
Boyd Cable
Bram Stoker
C. Collodi
C. E. Orr
C. M. Ingleby
Carolyn Wells
Catherine Parr Traill
Charles A. Eastman
Charles Amory Beach
Charles Dickens
Charles Dudley Warner
Charles Farrar Browne
Charles Ives
Charles Kingsley
Charles Klein
Charles Hanson Towne
Charles Lathrop Pack
Charles Romyn Dake
Charles Whibley
Charles Willing Beale
Charlotte M. Braeme
Charlotte M. Yonge
Charlotte Perkins Stetson
Clair W. Hayes
Clarence Day Jr.
Clarence E. Mulford
Clemence Housman
Confucius
Coningsby Dawson
Cornelis DeWitt Wilcox
Cyril Burleigh
D. H. Lawrence
Daniel Defoe
David Garnett
Dinah Craik
Don Carlos Janes
Donald Keyhoe
Dorothy Kilner
Dougan Clark
Douglas Fairbanks
E. Nesbit
E. P. Roe
E. Phillips Oppenheim
E. S. Brooks
Earl Barnes
Edgar Rice Burroughs
Edith Van Dyne
Edith Wharton

Edward Everett Hale
Edward J. O'Biren
Edward S. Ellis
Edwin L. Arnold
Eleanor Atkins
Eleanor Hallowell Abbott
Eliot Gregory
Elizabeth Gaskell
Elizabeth McCracken
Elizabeth Von Arnim
Ellem Key
Emerson Hough
Emilie F. Carlen
Emily Bronte
Emily Dickinson
Enid Bagnold
Enilor Macartney Lane
Erasmus W. Jones
Ernie Howard Pie
Ethel May Dell
Ethel Turner
Ethel Watts Mumford
Eugene Sue
Eugenie Foa
Eugene Wood
Eustace Hale Ball
Evelyn Everett-green
Everard Cotes
F. H. Cheley
F. J. Cross
F. Marion Crawford
Fannie E. Newberry
Federick Austin Ogg
Ferdinand Ossendowski
Fergus Hume
Florence A. Kilpatrick
Fremont B. Deering
Francis Bacon
Francis Darwin
Frances Hodgson Burnett
Frances Parkinson Keyes
Frank Gee Patchin
Frank Harris
Frank Jewett Mather
Frank L. Packard
Frank V. Webster
Frederic Stewart Isham
Frederick Trevor Hill
Frederick Winslow Taylor

Friedrich Kerst
Friedrich Nietzsche
Fyodor Dostoyevsky
G.A. Henty
G.K. Chesterton
Gabrielle E. Jackson
Garrett P. Serviss
Gaston Leroux
George A. Warren
George Ade
Geroge Bernard Shaw
George Cary Eggleston
George Durston
George Ebers
George Eliot
George Gissing
George MacDonald
George Meredith
George Orwell
George Sylvester Viereck
George Tucker
George W. Cable
George Wharton James
Gertrude Atherton
Gordon Casserly
Grace E. King
Grace Gallatin
Grace Greenwood
Grant Allen
Guillermo A. Sherwell
Gulielma Zollinger
Gustav Flaubert
H. A. Cody
H. B. Irving
H.C. Bailey
H. G. Wells
H. H. Munro
H. Irving Hancock
H. R. Naylor
H. Rider Haggard
H. W. C. Davis
Haldeman Julius
Hall Caine
Hamilton Wright Mabie
Hans Christian Andersen
Harold Avery
Harold McGrath
Harriet Beecher Stowe
Harry Castlemon
Harry Coghil
Harry Houidini

Hayden Carruth
Helent Hunt Jackson
Helen Nicolay
Hendrik Conscience
Hendy David Thoreau
Henri Barbusse
Henrik Ibsen
Henry Adams
Henry Ford
Henry Frost
Henry James
Henry Jones Ford
Henry Seton Merriman
Henry W Longfellow
Herbert A. Giles
Herbert Carter
Herbert N. Casson
Herman Hesse
Hildegard G. Frey
Homer
Honore De Balzac
Horace B. Day
Horace Walpole
Horatio Alger Jr.
Howard Pyle
Howard R. Garis
Hugh Lofting
Hugh Walpole
Humphry Ward
Ian Maclaren
Inez Haynes Gillmore
Irving Bacheller
Isabel Cecilia Williams
Isabel Hornibrook
Israel Abrahams
Ivan Turgenev
J.G.Austin
J. Henri Fabre
J. M. Barrie
J. M. Walsh
J. Macdonald Oxley
J. R. Miller
J. S. Fletcher
J. S. Knowles
J. Storer Clouston
J. W. Duffield
Jack London
Jacob Abbott
James Allen
James Andrews
James Baldwin

James Branch Cabell
James DeMille
James Joyce
James Lane Allen
James Lane Allen
James Oliver Curwood
James Oppenheim
James Otis
James R. Driscoll
Jane Abbott
Jane Austen
Jane L. Stewart
Janet Aldridge
Jens Peter Jacobsen
Jerome K. Jerome
Jessie Graham Flower
John Buchan
John Burroughs
John Cournos
John F. Kennedy
John Gay
John Glasworthy
John Habberton
John Joy Bell
John Kendrick Bangs
John Milton
John Philip Sousa
John Taintor Foote
Jonas Lauritz Idemil Lie
Jonathan Swift
Joseph A. Altsheler
Joseph Carey
Joseph Conrad
Joseph E. Badger Jr
Joseph Hergesheimer
Joseph Jacobs
Jules Vernes
Julian Hawthrone
Julie A Lippmann
Justin Huntly McCarthy
Kakuzo Okakura
Karle Wilson Baker
Kate Chopin
Kenneth Grahame
Kenneth McGaffey
Kate Langley Bosher
Kate Langley Bosher
Katherine Cecil Thurston
Katherine Stokes
L. A. Abbot
L. T. Meade

L. Frank Baum
Latta Griswold
Laura Dent Crane
Laura Lee Hope
Laurence Housman
Lawrence Beasley
Leo Tolstoy
Leonid Andreyev
Lewis Carroll
Lewis Sperry Chafer
Lilian Bell
Lloyd Osbourne
Louis Hughes
Louis Joseph Vance
Louis Tracy
Louisa May Alcott
Lucy Fitch Perkins
Lucy Maud Montgomery
Luther Benson
Lydia Miller Middleton
Lyndon Orr
M. Corvus
M. H. Adams
Margaret E. Sangster
Margret Howth
Margaret Vandercook
Margaret W. Hungerford
Margret Penrose
Maria Edgeworth
Maria Thompson Daviess
Mariano Azuela
Marion Polk Angellotti
Mark Overton
Mark Twain
Mary Austin
Mary Catherine Crowley
Mary Cole
Mary Hastings Bradley
Mary Roberts Rinehart
Mary Rowlandson
M. Wollstonecraft Shelley
Maud Lindsay
Max Beerbohm
Myra Kelly
Nathaniel Hawthrone
Nicolo Machiavelli
O. F. Walton
Oscar Wilde

Owen Johnson
P.G. Wodehouse
Paul and Mabel Thorne
Paul G. Tomlinson
Paul Severing
Percy Brebner
Percy Keese Fitzhugh
Peter B. Kyne
Plato
Quincy Allen
R. Derby Holmes
R. L. Stevenson
R. S. Ball
Rabindranath Tagore
Rahul Alvares
Ralph Bonehill
Ralph Henry Barbour
Ralph Victor
Ralph Waldo Emmerson
Rene Descartes
Ray Cummings
Rex Beach
Rex E. Beach
Richard Harding Davis
Richard Jefferies
Richard Le Gallienne
Robert Barr
Robert Frost
Robert Gordon Anderson
Robert L. Drake
Robert Lansing
Robert Lynd
Robert Michael Ballantyne
Robert W. Chambers
Rosa Nouchette Carey
Rudyard Kipling
Saint Augustine
Samuel B. Allison
Samuel Hopkins Adams
Sarah Bernhardt
Sarah C. Hallowell
Selma Lagerlof
Sherwood Anderson
Sigmund Freud
Standish O'Grady
Stanley Weyman
Stella Benson
Stella M. Francis

Stephen Crane
Stewart Edward White
Stijn Streuvels
Swami Abhedananda
Swami Parmananda
T. S. Ackland
T. S. Arthur
The Princess Der Ling
Thomas A. Janvier
Thomas A Kempis
Thomas Anderton
Thomas Bailey Aldrich
Thomas Bulfinch
Thomas De Quincey
Thomas Dixon
Thomas H. Huxley
Thomas Hardy
Thomas More
Thornton W. Burgess
U. S. Grant
Upton Sinclair
Valentine Williams
Various Authors
Vaughan Kester
Victor Appleton
Victor G. Durham
Victoria Cross
Virginia Woolf
Wadsworth Camp
Walter Camp
Walter Scott
Washington Irving
Wilbur Lawton
Wilkie Collins
Willa Cather
Willard F. Baker
William Dean Howells
William le Queux
W. Makepeace Thackeray
William W. Walter
William Shakespeare
Winston Churchill
Yei Theodora Ozaki
Yogi Ramacharaka
Young E. Allison
Zane Grey